father Panic's Opera Macabre

Also by Thomas Tessier

Fog Heart

Secret Strangers

Rapture

Finishing Touches

Phantom

The Nightwalker

Shockwaves

The Fates

Ghost Music and Other Tales

father Panic's
Opera Macabre

Thomas Tessier

Subterranean Press ⟫⟨ 2001

FIRST EDITION

January 2001

Limited edition ISBN

1-931081-12-3

Lettered edition ISBN

1-931081-13-1

Subterranean Press

P.O. Box 190106

Burton, MI 48519

email:

publisher@subterraneanpress.com

website:

www.subterraneanpress.com

for Anthony Glavin
poet, musician and friend
who, in numerous Dublin coffeehouses and pubs,
taught me English

and for Bora Bozic

The Cities send to one another saying:
'My sons are Mad
With wine of cruelty. Let us plat a scourge,
O Sister City.'
Children are nourish'd for the Slaughter;
once the Child was fed
With Milk, but wherefore now are Children
fed with blood?
The Horse is of more value than the Man.
The Tyger fierce
Laughs as the Human form;
the Lion mocks & thirsts for blood.
They cry, 'O Spider, spread thy web!
Enlarge thy bones & fill'd
With marrow, sinews & flesh,
Exalt thyself, attain a voice.

— WILLIAM BLAKE, *VALA*

1

The House
of Tiles

It was late in the afternoon when the Fiat overheated. Neil had watched with a growing sense of annoyance and anxiety as the temperature gauge edged slowly upward. He still had plenty of gas in the tank, but no coolant or even plain water for the radiator. It was the time of day when, in any event, he would be looking for a town with a small hotel or a guesthouse to stay at for the night, but the last village he'd passed through was nearly an hour behind him. Surely it would be better to continue on in this direction now. He was bound to find help somewhere soon, a town, a farmhouse at least — if his car would just hold up a little while longer.

Neil wasn't sure exactly where he was anymore, but he knew that he was probably still in the Marches, most likely in the Monti Sibillini, a range of mountains once thought to be the home of the sibyls of classical myth. The dominant peak in the near distance had to be Monte Vettore. Somewhere in this area was the Lago di Pilato, where according to legend Pontius Pilate was buried, perhaps even in the lake itself. Now and then Neil glimpsed another range farther off, which he assumed to be the Gran Sasso, part of the Apennines. Tomorrow, or as soon as the car was checked out and ready to run, Neil's route would take him in that direction, and eventually back to his apartment in Rome. A breakdown would be a minor nuisance, but he knew approximately where he was, and he wasn't lost.

This was Neil's second excursion since he had arrived in Italy, and he now felt quite comfortable driving around the country by himself. A couple of months ago he'd made the same kind of rambling tour of Tuscany. It was predictably beautiful and delightful, but perhaps a bit too familiar. Tuscany has been hosting visitors for centuries, its hill towns and byways have been endlessly written about, painted and photographed. Some of that must have seeped into Neil's mind over the years, via books, magazines, television and Italian films, because there had been moments when he felt the strange sensation of having already been in a certain town or village, though it was in fact his first visit to the region.

This time out he wanted to see some part of the country that was less well-traveled and not as heavily visited by outsiders, to avoid the obvious routes and hopefully to find here and there a little of the old Italy — assuming that it was still there to be found. A friend at the Academy had suggested that Neil try Abruzzo and the Marches, which proved to be a good idea.

He had driven east from Rome to Pescara, stopping only twice along the way. It was the shortest route to the Adriatic coast. From there he turned north and drove the A14 as far as Ancona, an uninteresting run that took him through one beach resort town after another. But when Neil finally left the *autostrada* behind and began to circle slowly inland, he soon found himself in exactly the kind of countryside he had been looking for. The land rose up steadily, wrinkling itself into steep hills and mountains. The roads were all narrow, frequently little more than country lanes that snaked along the rims of deep canyons and gorges, plunging, rising, curling unpredictably. The towns and small villages Neil passed through were perched on high cliffs, terraced along rippling hillsides, or nestled in tiny vales.

It would be inaccurate to describe the Marches as isolated or out of touch with the rest of the country and the world, but it was somewhat out of the way, and it was definitely a little rougher and wilder than any other part of Italy Neil had experienced so far. It was old, and in some villages almost the only people he saw were elderly, the young having moved elsewhere for college or jobs.

In some places there was nothing to see other than a few ramshackle old stone houses clustered around a small central square where old men sat outdoors, drinking wine, playing cards, chatting idly among themselves or dozing in the sun. Neil spoke Italian fairly well but he found it difficult to get a conversation going with these people. They were polite, but their reticence and open but distant stares reminded him — lest he forget for a moment — that he was an outsider among them.

The needle was just touching the red band at the far right side of the gauge now. Perhaps the car needed oil, not coolant. It didn't make much difference though, since he didn't have an extra quart of oil with him either. But he had checked both fluid levels before leaving Rome, so there had to be a leak somewhere in the system.

Neil had spent nearly a week meandering around the Marches now, from Loreto to San Leo, Gradara, Macerata, Camerino, Visso. He'd taken in some of the obvious sights like the Frasassi Caves and the Infernaccio Gorge, but for the most part what he liked best was simply wandering around the old towns, taking in forts and palazzos that dated back hundreds of years but were still quite impressive, gazing at art and architecture that survived from a time when the world was completely different, but still human, still ours. At such moments Neil could almost taste the past in his mouth and feel it on his skin. The phantom sensations of half-forgotten or lost history — it still amazed him that he was actually making a fairly successful career for himself out of these unlikely and insubstantial impressions.

Now he was in the emptier upper reaches of the province, a place of black stony tarns and ragged windswept grasslands, the whole laced through with sharp ridges, rocky outcroppings and narrow dark glens. The asphalt gave way more often to longer stretches of loose and rutted gravel. It was easy to suspect that you had strayed off the road and onto a rural path that had fallen into disuse and now led nowhere, but Neil had already learned that it wasn't necessarily so — it was just the way the roads were in this area.

Still, it happened to him now. The road dipped down and swung in a long arc around a high stone shelf. When he came out on the far side of it, he saw a large house and several low outbuildings on the hillside a few hundred yards ahead, and he could see that this was not a through road after all, that it ended at the house. No matter. Neil still felt a sense of relief. He would at least be able to get water for his car and directions back to the main road and the nearest town.

As Neil drove slowly closer, the road wound down through clumps of trees and stands of tall thick brush before rising again. His angle of view had changed so that when he finally came out into a clearing he was looking up at the house, and it suddenly exploded in dazzling light. It was catching the sun on its descent in the west, Neil realized. The house had looked a kind of dull buff color at first, but now it shimmered like burning gold.

The effect was so striking that Neil shifted into neutral and just stared at the house for a few moments. He noticed that the façade was covered with painted yellow tiles, scores of them, each about two feet square. The house was old, many of the tiles were chipped or cracked, but the clever light trick still worked. The person who conceived and built it had probably been dead for decades, but Neil silently said thanks — his pleasure disturbed only when he noticed steam billowing out from beneath the hood of the car.

2

Sticks and Strings

Neil turned the key and got out. He put the hood up to help the engine cool off faster. Now that he looked carefully at the radiator, he could see that it was in poor shape. The fins were corroded, and in places had completely rotted away. No real surprise there. He'd known it was an old car when he bought it from the art historian Lydia Margulies, who was just finishing her stay at the Academy when Neil arrived. But the car was a bargain, and it had not given him any trouble until now. Still, this was something he should have anticipated and taken care of before he left Rome.

He started walking toward the house. For a moment Neil wondered if it was one of the many abandoned farms that could be found across the Italian countryside. There were no signs of life and the only sound was the loud hiss of the strong breeze in the trees. Three large brick chimneys protruded from the red pantile roof, each containing four separate clay pipes, but no smoke came from any of them. He noticed that several of the individual roof tiles were cracked or had slipped.

But it occurred to Neil that if the house had been left derelict, most of the windows would surely be broken by now, and none of them were. It was a large boxy building, three stories high. The windows on the first two floors were tall, wide rectangles, but those at the top level were small and circular, almost like portholes, suggesting an attic with a low ceiling.

Neil found traces of a footpath as he approached the house — he could feel and see a bed of tiny white chipped stones beneath the thick coarse grass that had claimed most of the ground. There was a long balustrade marking off a terrace immediately in front of the house. It was made from a purplish-grey stone that Neil had seen elsewhere in the region. The same material had also been used for the weed-lined paving stones on the terrace and the broad steps that led up to the front door. A few stone urns graced the balustrade, but they held no ornamental shrubs or flowers.

As he passed along in front of the house, Neil hoped to see something through the windows, but the rooms inside were blocked from view by heavy drapes. The glass panes were coated with a thin layer of grime. Up close, he noticed that the impressive tiles covering the house looked merely faded and dull when the sun's rays didn't hit them at the right angle, their gloss muted with dust. Most of them were blank, simply colored yellow, but a few, seemingly placed at random, also contained rust-brown markings or motifs. They were unfamiliar to Neil but made him think of indecipherable runes, clotted Gothic lettering and dead Teutonic languages. He knew that there was still a strong Germanic presence farther north, particularly in the Italian alps, and that in Friulia there were people who spoke something that was neither modern German nor Italian, but a vestigial hybrid of old Low German and Roman Latin. So this house seemed out of place in the Marches, but that only pleased Neil. It was just the kind of unusual thing he'd hoped to find in his meandering explorations.

A somewhat larger yellow tile was centered directly above the front door. It contained a dark red sketch of a human head, seen in profile, drawn in a few bold strokes. It was crudely heroic but striking, and it suggested a prince or a warrior. He had a flowing moustache and wore a conical helmet from the Middle Ages. Then Neil noticed the man's eye. It should have been only partly visible on the left side of the head, as seen naturally in profile, but the entire eye had been sketched in. It was not turned forward with the rest of his face, but out, directly at anyone coming to the house. It was an anatomical impossibility that made Neil smile.

There was no bell or knocker, so he rapped his fist on the wooden door. After a minute or so, he tried again, longer this time, forcefully enough to hurt his knuckles. Still, no sound came from within. He pounded the door with the fleshy side of his fist, and then with the fat part of the palm of his hand, but again to no result. Finally, he decided he would have to go around to the back of the house and try to find someone there.

As Neil turned to walk down the steps, he was startled to see a child sitting on the balustrade, at the farthest end. A little girl, maybe eight or nine years old. Surely he hadn't failed to notice her as he approached the house. She must have come out and hopped up there while he was knocking on the door. Somebody is home, Neil thought gratefully.

The girl's short legs stuck out slightly in the air. She appeared to be playing with a puppet in the shape of man, made from sticks and string. She held her hand out and walked the puppet back and forth and in tight circles on the grey stone balustrade. Her head bobbed rhythmically and her lips moved as if she were talking or singing quietly to herself as she played.

Neil didn't want to frighten her so he smiled broadly to convey his friendliness. As he got closer he could hear her voice — it was surprisingly harsh, and she spoke in a language he didn't recognize. It sounded tangled, vaguely Slavic. With each step he took toward her, the tempo and volume of her speaking ratcheted up, as if she were narrating his harmless movements into an event of absurd tension and melodrama. It was the kind of silly thing that a dreamy child would do.

She wore a black skirt that came down to her ankles and heavy black shoes that looked too large for her feet. A man's plaid outdoors shirt hung loosely like a light jacket over her grimy sweatshirt. In the declining sun her hair appeared reddish-blonde, but it was matted in a thick frizzy clump. The sun was just above and behind her, almost directly in his line of vision, so it wasn't until Neil came within fifteen feet of her that he realized she was not a child at all. Far from it, she had to be at least forty — probably older. Several of her teeth were missing, the others stained or chipped. She had blotchy red cheeks, the skin around her mouth was lined and the flesh beneath her hooded eyes was purplish and sunken. But it was the crazed look of gleeful malice in those eyes that most disturbed Neil. His smile quickly faded away.

The woman's plump stubby fingers worked the sticks faster, making the puppet dance and jump wildly. She bounced up and down on her perch, and her voice was a loud mad rant. Neil said something in Italian but it had no effect on her. The poor woman probably suffered from some mental illness or defect, perhaps genetic in origin. He felt very uncomfortable in her presence and didn't know what to do next.

The puppet distracted him. In spite of his own reluctance, Neil found himself moving closer to peer at it. The stick figure was a little over a foot in height and had been fashioned as a human skeleton. But the bones and details were so well done that Neil realized it couldn't be made out of carved sticks, it had to be manufactured. Then he noticed the naturally misshapen skull, the toothless jaw, the tiny leathery pieces that might be tendons or gristle, and the dull brownish stains in certain parts of the bones.

The woman was laughing raucously, but then she suddenly froze in silence, as if a switch had been turned. Her eyes were staring blankly past Neil. Before he had time to react, she hopped off the balustrade and scurried away from him, around the side of the house and out of sight, the gruesome puppet dangling from her hand.

⇒3⇐

Mechanical fix

From the way the dwarf suddenly halted her strange act and stared past him, Neil knew that someone else had appeared. He turned back toward the house and was relieved to see a young woman standing alone at the top of the stone steps by the front door. Neil turned on the friendly smile again. In a relatively isolated spot like this he expected to be met with some caution or even unfriendliness. The dwarf had already unsettled him a bit, so he wanted to appear as harmless and unthreatening as he actually was. He held his arms out and opened his hands in a gesture of helplessness.

The woman came down to the bottom of the steps, and Neil stopped a few yards from her. She looked refreshingly normal in black designer jeans, a long-sleeved white blouse, stylish sunglasses and sandals. She didn't seem at all concerned, but merely perplexed by his presence.

Neil quickly explained the situation, pointing to his car. She nodded her head slowly while he spoke, as if she could not quite grasp his point. But then she stifled a big yawn and smiled sheepishly at him, and Neil realized that he had probably awakened her from an afternoon nap. He apologized for disturbing her, repeating that unfortunately his car could go no farther without water. He added that he would also be grateful for directions to the nearest town where he could find a room for the night. Now the woman seemed to be more awake and she gave a brief nod of comprehension.

"*Si, si. Acqua.*"

"*Si, grazie.*"

"I can tell from your pronunciation that you're an American," she then said in smooth, lightly accented English. "Am I right?"

"Ah, you speak English. Yes, you're right, I am American. I'm living in Rome for a year, as part of my work. I took some time off to drive around and explore the countryside. My name is Neil O'Netty, by the way."

"I'm Marisa Panic," she replied, pronouncing her last name *Pahn*-ik. "I'm pleased to meet you."

"And you." Neil gently shook her offered hand, which felt pleasantly cool and dry. "When I first came around the bend and saw the house, I was afraid there might not be anyone at home."

"Oh, we're always here. Onetti? That's Italian."

"O'Netty with a *y*," Neil explained. "It's Irish, but I am Italian on my mother's side, which is how I got a headstart on the language."

"I see. You do speak it well. And I think you're from Massachusetts. Somewhere in the Boston area?"

"Right again." Neil laughed. "Southie, then Medford."

"It's not that you have a very strong accent," Marisa told him. "But I spent a year at B.U. on a student exchange program."

"Aha." Neil was delighted. It had been a while now since he'd had a chance to converse in his own language. It felt comfortable and relaxing, like getting into his favorite old clothes. "Well, I think your English sounds better than my Italian."

"Thank you." She smiled. "I don't get to use it much here."

Neil found her very attractive. Marisa's skin was milky white, with a faint rosy glow, and she had long cascading waves of very fine black hair that was not glossy but had a rich, subdued luster, like polished natural jet. She was about 5'6" tall and her body was sleek but gloriously voluptuous. Neil wondered what color her eyes were — even through the sunglasses, he could see flashes of light in them.

"Are you still studying?" he asked.

"No, I finished last year. The University of Parma."

"Really? Parma is one of the cities I plan to visit while I'm here." It was true. He loved *The Charterhouse of Parma*, and Stendhal had, in a way, been an inspiration and a small factor in Neil's recent success.

"I can tell you a couple of good places to stay, clean, not expensive," Marisa said. "And some excellent family restaurants."

"Great. Thank you."

"Are you traveling alone or with — ?"

"Yes, I'm on my own."

"Let's see to your car. Then we can have some refreshments."

As they walked briskly toward the Fiat, Marisa clapped her hands sharply three or four times and called out a couple of words that Neil could not recognize. He saw a man emerge from one of the low worksheds on the nearest rise. Marisa shouted something else to him, and the man went back into the shed, reappearing a few moments later with a large plastic container and a funnel in his hands.

"What language were you speaking to him?"

"I'm not sure what you would call it," Marisa replied with a laugh. "These people have been with my family for a long time. It's some kind of local dialect from Dalmatia, I believe."

"Is your family Italian?"

"On my mother's side, like you. My father's family, well, they say if you go back far enough, they were the original Illyrians. I don't know any of that ancient history, but my grandfather and his family came here at the end of World War II, fleeing the Communists on the other side of the Adriatic. They bought this old farm, which had gone to ruin during the war."

They had arrived at Neil's car. The man came hurrying along a few seconds later. He had the rough, ruddy features and large leathery hands of somebody who had worked outdoors for decades, and he might have have been anywhere from forty to sixty years of age. His clothes were stained and torn, he had the same gnarly, raggedy appearance of the dwarf, but he was of average height and build. He ignored Neil and glanced subserviently toward Marisa as he set the plastic container and funnel down on the ground. He used a rag to remove the radiator cap, which was still hot to touch. Neil stepped closer to take a look. No liquid visible, as he feared.

Neil sat inside and turned the engine over, then got out again to hold the funnel while the man angled the bulky jug and carefully poured a small but steady stream of water into the radiator. Neil watched it swirl down through the funnel. A minute later, he could see it accumulating and moving inside as the pump circulated the liquid. The system took a lot of water, but finally the radiator was full.

"All right, now let's see," Neil said.

As soon as he put the cap on and snugged it tight, the pressure inside increased and tiny jets of water appeared in several places on the body of the radiator. Soon it was hissing audibly and the rising steam was visible in the air. The man pointed theatrically. Neil frowned.

"How far is it to the nearest town?"

"Four miles back to the road," Marisa said, "and about another eight miles from there. Your car wouldn't make that, would it?"

"I doubt it. Can I use your phone to call for a tow?"

"I'm afraid there's no telephone here," she answered with a look of apology. "My brother has a cell phone, but he's away on business until the end of the week."

"Could I trouble you to drive me to the town, and then I could make arrangements to have my car picked up?"

"My brother has the car too," Marisa replied with another look of sincere regret. "It's the only workable vehicle we have."

Neil's car was boiling out clouds of steam now. As he went to switch it off, Marisa started speaking quickly to the workman. It sounded like she was asking him something. He nodded and answered her at some length. She turned to Neil and smiled.

"He thinks the radiator is ruined."

Neil gave a short laugh. "I think he's right."

"But he thinks they can patch it up enough tomorrow so that you'll at least be able to get to town and replace it."

"Oh, that'd be great," Neil exclaimed, his spirits lifting. "Thank him for me, I'm really very grateful."

"Of course you'll stay here tonight."

"That's very kind of you. I'm sorry to impose on you like this. I hope it won't be too much of an inconvenience."

"Not at all," Marisa said, smiling brightly. "We have plenty of room, and I'm so glad to have some company for a change. Come on, get your bag, whatever you need, and we'll go inside."

4

The Box Room

"You mentioned something about working in Rome. What business are you in — banking, finance, technology?"

"No, nothing like that," Neil said with a smile. "I have a one-year fellowship at the American Academy. I'm doing some research for a book I'm working on. And also writing it, of course."

Marisa had slipped her arm through his as they walked. It was a common practice in many European countries, so Neil knew better than to read too much into her simple gesture. But he enjoyed the closeness and the physical contact with her.

"Ah, you're a writer."

"An author, yes."

"That's marvelous." Marisa gave his arm a little squeeze. "What kind of books do you write?"

"Historical fiction, sort of." Neil always felt a little awkward trying to explain his work. "Anyhow, I've only written three so far."

"But that's wonderful. They must be very good for you to be chosen for the Academy. It's very prestigious."

"The first two disappeared almost without a trace," Neil told her with a rueful smile. "But the last one did much better."

"What is it about, what period of history?"

"The 1590s, in Italy. It's called *La Petrella* and it's a retelling of the story of Beatrice Cenci and her family."

"Oh, of course. I remember that," Marisa said excitedly. "Beatrice conspired with her mother to murder her father, and she was then tortured and beheaded in public for it, even though her father had raped her. She was only about, what — fifteen years old?"

"That's right."

"It's a famous story."

"Yes, but not in America. I discovered that there hadn't been a full-length fictional treatment of it in many years, so I decided to try it. I found Beatrice by way of Nathaniel Hawthorne, who saw Guido's portrait of her in the Barberini Gallery and fell in love with her. I read Stendhal's account of the case, and many others. But my version is quite different."

"You changed the story?" Marisa asked.

"Not the facts or the incidents," Neil said. He felt that he was talking too much about something that could not really interest her. "But the feelings and motivations of the people. Beatrice is usually idealized, portrayed as an innocent, still virtually a child."

"Wasn't she?"

"I tried to make her both innocent and knowing," Neil said. "When I did more research and read some passages from the actual court documents of the case, I found it all much more uncertain and open to interpretation in different ways. There's a moral ambiguity to Beatrice, which is probably why she fascinates me."

"I see. But her father — he really was an evil man?"

"Oh yes, he was a monster."

That seemed to please Marisa, who smiled broadly. "I'd love to read your book."

"I'm sorry I don't have a copy with me, but I'll be happy to send you one when I get back to Rome."

"Thank you. Signed, please?"

"Of course."

Marisa squeezed his arm again and Neil smiled at her. She was so attractive, pleasant to talk to and be with, and his encounters with women had been disappointingly few since he'd come to Italy.

They reached the front door, but before she opened it Marisa turned and looked around as if she were checking the weather. Then she led him into a dimly-lit entrance hall. As soon as the door clicked shut, Neil noticed how quiet the house was. There were two large armoires and a couple of free-standing coat racks, along with a pair of heavy upholstered chairs made of very dark wood, and a long ornate wooden bench. All of this furniture was old, chipped and dusty. A gloomy corridor led straight into the house from the entrance area. Off to the right was a wide flight of stairs that led to a landing and then angled up toward the center again.

"I hope you won't mind waiting for a moment while I go and make arrangements for your room and bed? We so seldom have visitors, I want to make sure they open the window and change the linens."

"Don't go to any trouble for me," Neil insisted politely. "I'd be fine on a couch with a blanket."

"Oh no, we can certainly do better than that." Marisa led him into a small sitting room and turned on a floor lamp that had a battered shade with a fringe. "You can sit here. I'll be right back."

"Thank you."

As soon as he was alone, Neil noticed that it was an interior room. It had no windows, no other doors. There were two plain wooden chairs, both so dusty that he decided not to sit down. Boxes of old books were stacked up against the back wall of the narrow room. He went closer and looked at them but the titles were in a language he didn't recognize.

Neil began to feel uncomfortable in his breathing. He was asthmatic, though he had such a mild case of it that he rarely experienced difficulties. A single Benadryl capsule was usually enough to quell a reaction. But now he could taste powdery alkaline fungus in his mouth — even before he spotted the patches of it on the lower side walls of the room. Neil's lungs tightened, he could feel himself losing the ability to breathe in and out.

He turned toward the door, forcing himself to move slowly and carefully, as he had learned long ago — sudden exertions only made matters worse. Now he felt a little dizzy, lightheaded, as if he'd just been hit by a very powerful nicotine jag. This was something Neil didn't associate with asthma. His thoughts were foggy and vague, but he wondered if it was an effect of the particular fungus in that room — not mildew, it was something else, something new and deeply unpleasant to him — and he could imagine invisible toxic clouds of it being sucked in as he breathed, quickly absorbed into his blood, and then sluicing chaos into his brain.

Neil reached for the doorknob but his hand seemed to wave and flap listlessly in the air. Wow — the word formed in his mind with absurd calm and detachment — he couldn't remember the last time he had a reaction this strong and swift. He might even fall down.

But then Marisa opened the door and smiled at him.

5

Il Morbo

"You look pale," she said, taking his arm in hers again.

"I think I'm just a little tired, that's all," Neil said. "I did a lot of walking and driving today before I got here."

"Dinner is later, but we'll have some wine and snacks now."

"That sounds very good."

She led him down the long corridor toward the rear of the house. There were any number of doors on either side, but all of them were closed. They passed three more staircases, one that went down on the left side, then farther on another that went down to the right, and at the back, one more that led to the upper floors.

"Too many rooms," Marisa said, almost to herself. "It's impossible to take care of all these rooms anymore. Most of them are closed and never used. There's no need for them."

Neil nodded sympathetically. "Do you have any brothers or sisters? I mean, aside from the brother you mentioned."

"No, only Hugo. That's part of the problem. He's away on business often and has no interest in running things here. Neither do I," she added in a lower, almost conspiratorial tone.

A familiar story, Neil thought. He couldn't imagine someone like her remaining here for very long, even if it was her family home. A bright young woman who had recently finished her university degree — work and life and love were all to be found elsewhere now, out in the world.

He felt better as they stepped outside, his breathing was almost back to normal. They walked to a stone patio with a weathered wooden table and several chairs. It was located a short distance from the house, at an angle that allowed them a very attractive view of the sharp ridges and deep vales that unfolded in the distance.

He also saw, directly beyond the yard around the house, a gradually rising series of terraces and still more outbuildings. Men were working the plots, kids were playing, and Neil occasionally caught a glimpse of a woman in a woolly jacket and long skirt peering out of one hut or another.

He and Marisa sat at the table. A bottle of red wine and two crystal goblets had already been placed there, and two older women soon appeared to set down platters of food. Neil knew immediately from their features that they were not related to Marisa.

There were slices of cold sausage, black olives, cuts of three or four different kinds of cheese, something that looked like *pâte* or a meat pudding, a couple of loaves of bread, butter, a bowl of dark olive oil and a few jars and dishes that contained unknown sauces and spreads. The wine, which Marisa said they made from their own grapes, was a dark ruby-maroon in color and had a little too much of a tannic edge, but it was drinkable.

"*Robusto,*" Neil managed to say.

Marisa was no longer wearing sunglasses. Her eyes were deep blue, frank, open, curious — perhaps he was reading too much into them this soon, but they were so easy to gaze at. The breeze played in her silky black hair. She had such striking features — strong cheekbones, a wide mouth, rosy full lips, a proud nose, clear smooth skin with a pearly luster — altogether, they grabbed your attention and held it.

Neil and Marisa nibbled at the food, drank the wine and talked for an hour or more about books, history, Italy, America, and their lives. He felt very comfortable and relaxed with her. He was usually not one to volunteer much information about himself, but he soon found that he wanted to tell her things, that he enjoyed her questions and interest.

When *La Petrella* was published and Neil had to give quite a few interviews, he quickly developed a brief biographical sketch that satisfied most questioners. How he had stayed on in Worcester after graduating from Assumption College. The six years of substitute teaching by day, bartending nights and weekends at the Templewood Golf Course or at Olivia's. All of the reading and writing he had done in odd hours, slowly accumulating the first novel, and then the second. How both of those books were indifferently reviewed in only a few places, and barely sold. How Neil had decided to give fiction one more chance, and — bingo. The glowing reviews of *La Petrella,* the solid sales, the trade paperback that sold even better, and the film option. It was a happy American story, neat and edifying.

But with Marisa, Neil wanted to say more. He told her about the death of his mother, which was followed only a few months later by the breakup with his longtime girl-friend, Jamie, and how those two events had forever changed him, diminishing his expectations of life and instilling in him a certain resignation to melancholy that even now, almost four years later, showed no sign of going away.

"Ha, it serves her right," Marisa said of Jamie. "She left you just before your book came out and did so well. I'm sure she has kicked herself many times since then. Better you found out sooner than later. You should be glad she left when she did."

He wasn't, but Neil laughed at Marisa's words and part of him hoped that she was right about Jamie kicking herself. Still, even after the book was published, she had never called or written, never made any attempt to revive the relation-ship, and he'd long ago accepted the fact that it was dead.

Marisa spoke softly but quickly, her voice fluid and pleasing to the ear. She had a way of filling any brief moments of silence that arose. Neil gradually learned more about her, and it was pretty much as he had already guessed. She had returned home after college, intending to stay for a month or two, the summer at most. Her degree was in his-tory, which meant that she could only teach or go back to college for a postgraduate degree, neither of which appealed to her. She had been thinking of moving to Florence. She could always find a job like waitressing to earn money while she looked for an opening in a more interesting line of work — perhaps fashion, magazines, the arts. Florence was a lively creative city, there were always opportunities for bright young people who looked for them.

But she soon was caught up in "keeping things going" at home. Her parents and two surviving grandparents were all in varying stages of illness or frailty. It was impossible just to walk away. Her family and the tenants needed her. Marisa's brother Hugo was often away on business — he was a rep for a medical supply company — and his financial contributions were very helpful to the household.

Marisa seemed to understand that the whole enterprise was by now hopelessly outmoded, a relic of the past, and doomed to collapse, though she didn't say so. But she apparently regarded it as her family duty to do her part and see it through as long as her parents and grandparents were alive. As she spoke of these things, Neil could see that she was forcing herself to smile and affect a light tone, but there was loneliness and sadness in her eyes. It wasn't hard to understand why she was so grateful for a visitor.

Neil noticed a group of six or seven men standing together on one of the terraces. They appeared to be watching him, and Marisa. Neil wondered what those people would do when the farm finally went under. Perhaps they thought he was from the bank, and wondered the same thing. Even at some distance, they seemed alien, slightly wild, lost people.

A heavy mist was drifting across the hills and settling around them, a low grey cloud of moisture. It came with surprising swiftness, obscuring the sunset and the views. Marisa frowned.

"*Il morbo,*" she said.

"What?"

"This fog. It's a regular feature of the region, especiallly up here at these altitudes. The local people call it *il morbo.*"

Neil shivered, feeling a sudden chill. "That means sickness, illness, the plague," he said.

"Yes, exactly." Marisa laughed. "Sometimes it blows through and is gone in an hour, but it can linger for a couple of days — and when it does, you do start to think of it as a plague."

On the terrace above, the men were losing their individual definition in the mist, becoming a cluster of dark shadow figures. The air was grey and full of floating globules of wetness.

"Let's go inside," Marisa said.

6

Passegiata

She led him up a flight of stairs and along a short corridor. They took a sharply angled turn, so that they appeared to be heading back the way they had just come, though by a different passage. They went through a doorway, across a raised gallery that was open above an empty room, and then into yet another corridor. Their footsteps made an echoing hollow clatter on the bare floorboards. The floor itself seemed to tilt slightly one way and then another, or to sag in the middle — it was never quite solid and level.

Marisa held his arm snugly against her as they walked, and Neil could feel the movements of her hip. The way their bodies touched, the way Marisa smiled at him — he wanted to believe she was seriously flirting with him, but he decided it wasn't serious. Not yet, anyway. Now that they were indoors, he noticed a sweet woodsy fragrance about her. Juniper? Whatever it was, he found it deliciously attractive.

"The layout is a bit crazy," she said apologetically. "At one time we had many relatives living with us here — cousins, aunts, uncles, in-laws. The rooms were divided and altered many times over the years to accommodate everybody and their belongings."

"I see."

"There was a story that a couple of hundred years ago this was not a farmhouse, that it was originally a monastic retreat or home for some obscure religious order that eventually dwindled away."

"Is that right?"

"You can still see religious carvings and symbols in certain places on the old woodwork, so maybe it's true."

"I like places with a mysterious history," Neil said.

"Yes, so do I, but now it's just a big nuisance."

They turned a corner and were in a wider area, a cul-de-sac. There were two doors, one on either side of the dead-end wall. Marisa opened one of them and went into the room. Neil followed.

"I hope this will be all right," she said.

The room was large, almost square in shape, and sparsely furnished, but it looked comfortable enough. The tall narrow window was swung open and the air in the room was clear, with no trace of mustiness — that was the most important thing as far as Neil was concerned.

"Oh, this is fine," he said. "Very nice."

"There's a bathroom just outside, through the other door. Perhaps you'd like a little time now to unpack your things, to rest and wash up before dinner," she suggested.

"Yes, I would."

"I'll come back for you in, say, an hour and a quarter? I don't want you to get lost wandering around this place alone."

Neil laughed. "Again, I'm sorry to impose on you like this. I'm very grateful for your kind hospitality."

"It's no trouble at all." Marisa hesitated, or lingered, for a moment in the open doorway, smiling warmly at him before she turned to leave. "Make yourself at home here. I'll see you again in a little while."

He smiled back at her. "I look forward to it."

Neil stood and listened as the sound of her footsteps faded away, and then he surveyed the room again. There was a queen-size bed with ornate dark woodwork, an armoire, a chaise and one other chair, a clothes rack and a couple of small end tables. A bedside lamp and a standing floor lamp provided the only light, but they would do. A threadbare rug covered much of the plank floor. The walls were bare, and had been whitewashed so long ago that they had turned grey. He noticed an unlabeled brown bottle and two drinking glasses on one of the tables. He removed the glass stopper from the bottle, took a sniff, poured a few drops and tasted it — grappa. He splashed a little more in the glass. A nice touch.

45

Neil went to the window, rested his arms on the stone casement and leaned forward to look outside. He suddenly realized that his room was in a wing that had been added on to the main body of the house at some point. It was toward the rear of the house and on the far side, which explained why he hadn't noticed it either when he first approached the place or later, when he was sitting on the patio. Directly below him now, a drop of almost thirty feet, there was only a narrow curling path of ground between the house and the rim of a deep rocky gorge.

Neil finished the grappa and set his small travel alarm for forty-five minutes. He took off his shoes and stretched out on the bed. The mattress was soft and comfortable, and the large down pillows were lightly scented with cedar. Neil shut his eyes and dozed off almost immediately. When the alarm beeped he got up, gathered a few things and went into the bathroom. There was a huge old tub, a toilet with a water tank above it, a sink and mirror. The stone tile floor felt cold through his socks. Neil washed his face, shaved quickly, brushed his teeth and changed shirts. He felt better, clean and awake again, refreshed by the nap.

As Neil stepped back into his room, he heard a noise. It struck him, because until now he hadn't heard any sounds in the house other the ones he and Marisa made walking. This sound was raspy and grating, repeated in a steady rhythm, as if one piece of metal was being scraped against another. It sounded quite close by, so Neil walked the short distance into the corridor to see if he could find where and what it was. He still had a few minutes before Marisa was due to come and fetch him. Neil vowed not to embarrass himself by getting lost.

It was almost completely dark outside and very little light penetrated this inner corridor. He saw a few widely spaced electric candles mounted in sconces on the wall, but they were not turned on and there was no switch to be found in the immediate area. To make matters worse, once he was in the corridor Neil could not get a true sense of direction on the metallic noise. It was still there, somewhere around him, but elusive.

As his eyes slowly adjusted to the gloom, he began to discern a very faint shaft of light not too far down the passage to his right. Good enough, he thought. He would check it out and then return to his room.

Neil was still wearing only socks on his feet. The floorboards felt weak in places, almost spongy, and they groaned softly beneath his weight. It would be a real surprise if dry rot and woodworms hadn't already taken over large portions of the interior of the house, particularly in the rooms that were closed and unused, dark and damp.

The light came from a recess in the wall. Four steps led in and up to a landing with a wooden ceiling so low that Neil had to bow his head slightly when he got to it. There was a very small open area on the right, an alcove with a narrow built-in bunk. The pale light came from several votive candles in blue glass jars that stood in a line along a single wall shelf.

There was a young man lying in the bunk. He looked to be a teenager still, certainly no older than twenty. His skin was clear, his features boyish, his hair cut short and neatly arranged. A red sheet covered him from his feet to his chin. A stark iron crucifix was mounted on the wall directly above the boy's head. The skeletal Christ figure looked like it might have been carved out of ivory that had turned brownish-yellow.

Neil stood there for a moment, taking all this in, trying to imagine an explanation. He stepped closer and studied the youth. There was no sign of breathing — in fact, the boy's skin looked icy blue, though that was probably an illusion caused by the glass candleholders. Neil took one candle and held it below the boy's cheek, illuminating his face with a clear light. Oddly, all that did was make the blueness more apparent.

Unlikely possibilities flashed through Neil's mind. The boy had just died and was laid out here as at a wake. But why wouldn't Marisa tell Neil about it? Even more to the point, why would they put the body up here in this absurd little raised alcove instead of a proper sitting room downstairs, or the nearest funeral home? That made no sense. Perhaps the young man had died some time ago, and the family knew a way to preserve his body more or less perfectly, as it now appeared. But that seemed no less implausible.

Neil leaned forward and lightly pressed the back of his hand against the young man's gleaming forehead. It felt very cold and hard. When Neil took his hand away he saw a clear rosy-whitish impression of his fingers on the boy's skin. It disappeared in a second or two, heat vanishing.

Then Neil thought he heard a faint exhalation, and he became aware of the metal noise again, rasping somewhere nearby. He stumbled back, his socks slipped and he had to grab the wall to keep from falling on the stairs. Neil returned quickly to his room.

7

Pockets

Neil had no time to think about what he had just seen before he heard Marisa's heels clicking loudly down the corridor. She appeared in his open doorway, a sudden irresistible vision. She looked gorgeous. She was wearing a fashionable short, tight, sleeveless black dress with a scooped neckline. It was a dress perfectly designed to emphasize the generous curves and elegant lines of her splendid body.

It was impossible not to stare at her — Neil realized he was probably gaping like a teenage boy. But it also occurred to him that she had obviously chosen to dress like this for him and no one else in this place. Marisa's body filled his vision — it seemed to fill the entire barren room with the explosive richness of life.

She knocked needlessly on the door frame. That was when he finally noticed the smile on her face — playful, expectant.

"You look lovely," he told her.

"Did *signore* try his bed?"

"Yes, he did."

"And was it satisfactory?"

"Yes, it was very...comfortable."

"You're quite sure?" Mock-doubtful.

"Well, I think so."

"Nothing else you need?"

"Now that you're here, I'm fine."

She laughed. "That little rest did you some good, I'm thinking. You don't look so tired now."

"I do feel much better. Refreshed."

"Good, I'm glad. Are you ready to go downstairs?"

"Sure."

Neil put on his sports jacket and Marisa took his hand in hers as they left the room. She startled him by turning to the right in the corridor, so they were bound to walk right past the steps leading up into the alcove. He was even more surprised when she stopped at the entrance and turned as if to go up the steps — but there were no steps, only an open doorway into another room, this one quite small, with a circular staircase down to the ground floor. He must have misjudged the distance, he told himself. The stairs and alcove must be a little farther along that corridor. Neil almost asked Marisa about the dead boy, but decided not to for the time being.

Now they were in a large warmly lit room that featured a regulation size English billiards table. There were several overstuffed armchairs off on either side of the room. At the far end, a sofa and a couple more chairs were arranged around a portable television set. The billiards table was in quite good condition, complete with string pockets, but the rest of the furniture was the same kind of battered old junk he'd seen elsewhere in the house.

"Do you play?" Marisa asked.

"I have played pool, but not proper billiards."

"I'll teach you later, if you want. It's not hard to learn. The rules, I mean. The game itself is another matter."

"I'd like to learn." As long as she was teaching.

"This is the room where Hugo and I kind of hang out," she explained as she went to a small bar near the television set. "He likes to play billiards, so I learned just to give him some competition. Not that I'm very good. One of my uncles was crazy about the game and had this table shipped here from Paris. He died several years ago. The television gets two or three channels on a good night."

Neil nodded sympathetically, but he didn't know quite what to say. It all seemed so dreary and depressing. Even this large room, with its clutter of furniture and its warm lamps, where at least two people spent some time and relaxed, somehow still felt dark, empty and lonely, bereft of life. Only family love and loyalty could keep somebody in a place like this, but even allowing that Marisa had an abundance of those qualities, Neil thought she was bound to go batty sooner or later if she stayed here for very long.

"The table is beautiful," Neil said lamely.

Marisa poured two glasses of wine and gave one to him — the same house red, he discovered when he took a sip. Either he was getting used to it or this was a better bottle, because he found it more agreeable now. Marisa perched herself on the fat arm of a heavy armchair, her legs open to the extent that her dress would allow. Neil's throat tightened and his heart felt like it was booming in his chest.

Jamie had a somewhat fulsome figure too, at first, though in time she had become obsessive about taking off weight. Perhaps that was part of the big fuzzy why — why it all went wrong for them.

"There are a couple of things I should warn you about."

"Oh?"

"Nothing serious." Marisa smiled. "It's just that my relatives are all still pretty much old world people. By old world I mean, you know — before the War. That was the world they grew up in and they still have a lot of those ways and attitudes. They might seem rather —"

She hesitated, unable to find the word she wanted. "Different?" Neil offered. He was the writer.

"Yes." Marisa smiled gratefully. "Different."

"Thanks for telling me," he said. "But I'm sure it won't be a problem as far as I'm concerned. I'm always glad to have the chance to meet and talk with people who lived through that period."

"Good." Marisa was still hesitating about something. "Oh, and if you don't like the food, please, you don't have to eat it. Just have some bread and salad, and I'll fix you something else later. I can tell them we had a lot to eat on the patio earlier."

"We did, and I'm not that hungry now." Neil resisted the urge to smile at her warning about the food. "But I'm sure it'll be fine."

"Thank you."

"Not at all. I'm the guest here."

"One more thing."

"Yes?"

Marisa stood up and stepped close to him. The thin gold bracelets on her wrist gleamed in the light as she put her glass down on the bar. A vibrant blue opal the size of a quarter dangled from a black ribbon that hung tightly at the base of her slender throat. How he wanted to kiss that throat.

All of that lovely black hair, the fire in her eyes, the silky texture of her skin, the way her perfume seemed to settle around him and draw him still closer to her, the movement of her tongue moistening her lips just as she was about to speak — Neil was completely captivated by her physical presence, dazed by its power. Dazed, but still aware.

"I hope you don't mind, but I told them that you are a friend of mine from the university. Well, you're a little older, so I said you were a visiting lecturer there and we became acquaintances. That was rather naughty of me, I know. I should have spoken with you about it first."

"Oh," Neil said. "But, why?"

"Like I said, they're kind of funny that way. If they thought you were a stranger, they'd sit up awake all night, worrying, wondering — who is this man, who sent him, what does he really want? Where they came from and what they went through, a stranger at the door — you have no

53

idea how much it could disturb them. It's crazy, I know, but I thought it best not to risk upsetting them, at their age." Her eyes peered up at Neil, her expression submissive and childlike. "I'm sorry."

"That's all right." Now Neil allowed himself to touch her, putting his arm around her shoulder, stroking her back soothingly. "I understand and I'm sure you're right that it's better for them this way."

"Oh, thank you so much."

"Besides, I really was a teacher for a while."

Marisa smiled brightly, her body resting against his, her head on his chest. God, her hair felt so good on his cheek. He felt her hand on the small of his back. She looked up at him again and opened her mouth as he leaned forward to kiss her. Marisa's tongue met his aggressively, her arm tightened across his back and pulled him closer. Neil could feel the same anxious desire and tension in her body that simmered within him. Their kiss was long and deep, lingering. Finally, Marisa pulled her head back a couple of inches. Now her smile was intimate, complicitous. She slowly ran the tip of her finger along her wet lips.

"Well, hello."

"Hi..."

"We'd better go in now," she said.

"Mmm?" Neil kissed her neck and throat. Marisa sighed with pleasure, but then gently put her hands on his chest.

"Really. My uncle is a priest. If he were to walk in and find us like this, I'd never hear the end of it."

Neil must have frowned or pouted. Marisa kissed him consolingly, her tongue teasing him.

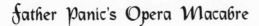
"Be patient," she said. "We must."

"Okay," he said, smiling. "Let's go."

Marisa took his hand and led him through a doorway into an empty enclosed passage that led to another door. When she opened it, the first thing Neil heard was the familiar sound of metal scraping on metal.

8

Gastronomico

There were six people already in the dining room when Marisa and Neil entered. They were seated at one end of a table that could hold twelve or fourteen. They were all elderly and they looked half-asleep, propped up in their chairs, barely moving until Marisa approached and spoke to them or touched them on the shoulder. Neil held back a few steps. He couldn't understand what Marisa was saying but the gentle affection in her voice was clear enough. There were three men and three women — Marisa's parents and grandparents, he learned. Neil stepped forward and smiled and nodded to each of them when Marisa gestured toward him.

They glanced briefly and vacantly at him, but none of them nodded or said anything. Handshakes were obviously not on.

One of the grandmothers had several small spoons on the table beside her plate, and she was sharpening them with a metal file. Neil stared at this curious spectacle for a few seconds before the old woman suddenly grinned at him and made a crisp scooping motion with the spoon she held.

"Fruit spoons," Marisa explained with a laugh. "You know, like for eating grapefruit with?"

"Oh, yes." Neil still couldn't imagine how he had been able to hear this persistent but not loud sound all the way upstairs. Yet he had no doubt that it was indeed the very same sound.

"Grandmother sharpens them every evening," Marisa explained, as if it were a perfectly normal activity. "It's one of the few things she can still do around the house, so I suppose it makes her feel a little bit useful."

"That's good for her, then." And perhaps it was, but Neil had never heard of anyone sharpening fruit spoons before. He took it to be an unusual but harmless display of eccentricity.

"Yes, it is." Marisa smiled gratefully.

The room was large, but aside from the table and chairs the only other furniture was a sideboard adjacent to the other door, which apparently led to the kitchen. The two long walls were hung with tapestries so faded and dusty that it was impossible for Neil to make out the scenes depicted on them. The room was lit only by candles, which didn't help. The wooden floor was bare and it sagged or tilted in places, just as it did elsewhere in the house.

The same two women who had served them on the patio now came into the room with bowls and platters of food. Marisa asked Neil to help her pour the wine, and he was grateful to have something to do. The men, who wore stiff, old-fashioned suits that almost resembled uniforms, exchanged a few quiet words with each other and then laughed briefly. Neil sensed that it was at his expense — perhaps they thought it absurd or humiliating that he let himself do a servant's work. And at a woman's bidding, no less. Not that he cared in the least about such a silly, anti-quated attitude. He also noticed the women casting gnomic glances at him, but they remained silent.

A place had been set at the head of the table, though no one occupied that chair. Neil hesitated, uncertain whether he should pour wine in the glass there too, but then Marisa nodded yes.

"My uncle — ah, here he is."

The priest came in through the doorway from the billiards room — Neil noted — and walked briskly to the table. He had wiry grey hair that was cut short. Although he looked nearly seventy he stood tall and straight and he had a sturdy, muscular build that conveyed strength and energy. The standard collar and black jacket made him look like just another diocesan priest, but he also wore a purple sash across his tunic, a medallion of the Virgin Mary, and there were several small pins and medals affixed to his lapels and breast pocket. He smiled and kissed Marisa lightly on the cheek.

"Father Anton, this is my friend Neil O'Netty from America," Marisa said, introducing them. "Neil, this is my uncle, Anton Panic."

"I'm very pleased to meet you," Neil said.

"Thank you, thank you. So nice." The priest's head bobbed several times and he clasped Neil's hand tightly. "So nice. Thank you."

Father Anton's eyes danced behind thick lenses, and Neil wondered if the frames could actually be genuine bakelite.

"Thank you, and your family, for your hospitality," Neil said to the priest, sensing that Father Anton was the decisive figure in the household. "I'm very grateful."

"No, please. Our pleasure to have a guest."

Neil and Marisa sat opposite each other, in the eighth and ninth places at the table. One of the servant women carefully set down a large covered porcelain tureen on the table between Neil and Marisa, and then left. Neil bowed his head slightly when he saw everyone else do that, and Father Anton said Grace in Latin, adding a few more words at the end in the family's other language. The old men chorused "Amen" loudly, and then laughed again, as if at a private joke.

Food was passed around. Neil loaded up on bread and salad, as Marisa had suggested. The bread was coarse and crusty, with a fresh yeasty smell. The salad contained various greens, mushrooms, peppers, tomatoes and chunks of cold meat sausage. Neil drizzled dark olive oil and balsamic vinegar on it. He also took a helping of a soupy rice dish.

The old man beside Neil nudged him in the arm. Neil assumed this was Marisa's father, though in fact he looked only marginally younger than the two grandfathers. He must have been in his early fifties when Marisa was born, but late births were probably not unusual on remote farms. It was clear that the man wanted Neil to help himself from the tureen now. He glanced at Marisa, who nodded reluctantly.

"But we can skip it," she said quickly.

"Oh. Well, let's see."

"You can just pass it along to them."

"That's all right."

Neil didn't want to appear rude. Even as Marisa was speaking to the others, apparently explaining how much she and Neil had eaten just a little while ago on the patio, he lifted the lid of the tureen. It appeared to be some kind of stew, brownish in color. Neil took the iron ladle and swirled it once through the liquid, stirring up small bits of meat, potatoes and — skulls. Tiny skulls that must have been very young birds, probably baby chickens. There were scores of them in the stew, each one roughly the size of a misshapen marble. O-kay. Neil smiled wanly at Marisa.

"I think you were right."

As soon as Neil lifted the heavy tureen and passed it along the table, the others broke into jolly laughter, and it felt as if some tension went out of the air. They were all fully awake now.

"I'm sorry, I warned you," Marisa said. "I wasn't sure, but I thought it might be something like that. Old tastes. It's an old recipe."

"That's okay," Neil assured her. "It's probably quite good, but I think I'd have to get myself in the right state of mind to try it."

"Mr. O'Netty," the priest spoke up. "Zuzu informed me that you have written a book about the case of Beatrice Cenci. Yes?"

"Zuzu is a family nickname for me," Marisa told him. "Don't ask me what it means, but it goes back to when I was a baby."

"I like it." Then he turned toward Father Anton. "Yes, that's right, my last novel was about the Cencis."

"Aha."

The priest spoke English slowly and with difficulty, but he was eager to hear about Neil's version of the story. He seemed particularly concerned that Neil might have been critical of Pope Clement VIII, for refusing to spare young Beatrice's life. Neil babbled on about what a thorny moral problem that was, even in today's world, and how he tried not to take one side or the other. A novel was not a debate, et cetera — the usual points he had made in numerous interviews. It was strange, speaking past six people who couldn't understand a word he was saying and ignored him. But Father Anton nodded every few seconds and appeared to be listening carefully.

Neil thought he was probably speaking for too long, but he couldn't focus his mind. His words seemed to vanish immediately in the air, and the only thing he could hear — on and on — was the muffled crunching sound of all those little bird skulls being eaten.

⇒9⇐

Billiards at Half-Past Ten

To Neil's relief, dinner in that house was a functional matter, not a social event. Marisa's parents and grandparents ate energetically and loudly, but surprisingly quickly. They drank one large glass of wine each, and when they were finished they shuffled off out of the room, scarcely even glancing at him as they left. It was probably his fault, Neil thought. If he weren't there, they would chat and linger at the table as families do — or did.

Though somehow he doubted that. The priest, Marisa and Hugo were the practical, capable ones who kept things going here. Without their efforts, the farm would be sold and the old folks packed off to a nursing home. Not that they seemed to appreciate it. Neil thought they acted as if they took all this for granted, which amounted to a terrible ingratitude. But — old people, old ways. They weren't going to change now.

When the others left, Father Anton came and sat beside Neil. He had a few more questions to raise and points to make about history and literature, which was apparently a matter of some real interest to him. Neil did his best to speak sensibly and not get carried away. He had no special theories or insights. History was interesting, it provided useful plots and frameworks as well as a magical sense of distance, of stepping into another world, another time and place. He felt very comfortable with it.

But all Neil really wanted to do was write tales that were like operas — gaudy, full of intensity, screaming emotion, high drama, sudden action, and troubled characters driven by primal human desires. That was the big stuff, as he thought of it. History itself wasn't the point. The critics had seen much more in *La Petrella* than Neil thought was there, including a few mysterious literary techniques he didn't even understand. Which made him feel kind of like a secret phony at times, but that was their business.

Father Anton was polite and intelligent, and after ten minutes he got up, clasped Neil's hand again, and said goodnight. He went around the table to kiss "Zuzu" on the forehead, and then left the room.

"He likes you," Marisa said. "I can tell."

"He seems very nice. But why is he living here? I mean, priests are usually assigned to parishes or schools," Neil added.

"He could be retired if he wanted, at his age. But he is on a kind of sabbatical instead. He is working on a paper for the Pope."

"Really?"

"Oh yes. Father Anton has known every pope, going back to Pius. He found a place at the Vatican early in his priesthood, and ever since then he has been very, you know what I mean, well-connected."

"Wow. What is his paper about?"

Marisa shrugged. "I'm not sure. Something to do with the history of conversions in Christianity. That's why he was so keen to hear what you had to say about how you make use of history in your books."

"Ah, I see."

The two servant women entered the room then and began to gather up the dishes and utensils. Neil thought he saw a sudden darkening of Marisa's expression. Then she turned to him, and smiled again. She pushed her chair away from the table and stood up.

"Shall we get out of the way?"

"Absolutely."

They went back into the billiards room. Marisa asked Neil to pour some more wine for both of them. She turned on the television and fiddled with the rabbit ears until she got a reasonably stable picture. It looked like some awful game show, but she turned the volume off. Then Marisa went to a shelf and picked up a pocket transistor radio that looked about forty years old. She rolled the little tuning wheel until she found a station playing some Abba-like Europop. The relentlessly cheerful tinny sound hung in the air like a bouquet of desiccated flowers.

"They aren't necessary for me," Neil said, nodding toward the radio and the television as he handed Marisa a glass of wine.

"I know, but it looks good. In case."

"In case?"

"You know. If someone comes in on us."

"You really think they would?"

"It's possible." Marisa shrugged, her eyes sad. "Better to give them a little while to get to bed."

"You're a grown woman."

"Don't make fun." Marisa turned away, pouting. "You can see that they don't think that way. They never will."

Neil put his drink down on the bar and stepped close behind her. He put his arms around her and kissed her hair and neck. "I'm sorry. I wasn't making fun. It's hard for you here, isn't it?"

She seemed to sigh and relax a little in his embrace. She gave a slow nod and her free hand reached around to rest on his hip. Neil's hands spread across her belly. When they brushed up against her breasts he felt her quick intake of breath, then the long slow exhalation, a vibration within her body, a silent cry of pleasure and deep need.

Marisa slipped out of his arms, turned around and leaned close to kiss him. Her tongue danced and teased, licking across his lips. She pressed her hand to his chest, as if to hold him back at a certain distance, but two fingers slipped between the buttons and touched his skin. She was smiling brightly again. Then her fingers tightened on his shirt and pulled him closer for one more kiss before she moved to the sofa.

"Let's sit," Marisa said. "Just for a little while."

"Okay."

They sat just a couple of feet apart on the sofa, their bodies turned to face each other. Neil caught a glimpse of Marisa's pearl grey panties and he realized that her legs were bare. It occurred to him that all of this might be a colossal tease and nothing more, but he doubted it, and in any event he didn't care if it was. Would he rather be alone in his room upstairs, trying to finish Rose Tremain's *Restoration?* Uh, no.

"So, tell me, why haven't you found someone else?" she asked. "It has been some time since this other woman left. A handsome young author like you, and very successful. I think the women would be knocking on your door day and night."

Neil laughed. He knew he was quite ordinary looking. But it was true that after the publication of *La Petrella* some women he'd known only on a casual social basis suddenly seemed to find him much more fascinating and worthy of their attention. Not to mention the strangers.

"I haven't been a monk."

"Aha."

"But no one serious." It was time to turn the tables. "And what about you? I can't believe you didn't have plenty of boyfriends when you were at college, in Parma."

"*Boys,* yes," Marisa said dismissively. "Anyhow..."

Neil watched the way her lips moved as she took another sip of wine, the slight tightening of the muscles in her throat as she swallowed. It was not unlike a fairy tale, he thought, or a romantic opera. Marisa was the beautiful young princess imprisoned in a remote castle by the evil queen or king, in this case by a whole van-load of elderly relatives and a bunch of tenant farmers. And that made Neil the prince who comes to rescue her, et cetera. It was the kind of old-fashioned story he liked — but it only took another momentary flash of sadness in Marisa's eyes to remind him that it was a very different matter for her, with no easy alternatives or solutions.

Still, there was nothing he could do. Invite her to Rome? Offer to take her with him when his car was fixed and he left? Sure, he could do that without any commitment on his part, but he sensed that Marisa would simply decline the offer. She had intelligence, spark, wit, and a desire to escape, but she also seemed resigned to play out the role that had been assigned to her for now by family and circumstance.

Her free hand rested across the inside of her thigh and her hair curled around her face, tumbling down over her shoulders like a gauzy wimple. She glanced at the door to the dining room and then back the other way toward the circular staircase. She leaned closer to Neil — who let his gaze linger on her cleavage. By now he was convinced that Marisa liked him looking at her this way, with voyeuristic intensity and undisguised desire.

They continued chatting for a few minutes but Neil was hardly aware of what they actually said. It was nothing important, just talk intended to pass whatever amount of time it took for Marisa to feel comfortable.

At one point she went to get the wine bottle from the bar. When she came back to the sofa, she sat right next to him. Their knees touched and she let her hand rest lightly on his leg. It was all Neil had been waiting for, the final signal. He ran the back of his fingers over her cheek, then trailed them down to stroke the inner curves of her breasts, her skin so silky and lovely to touch. Her hand moved between his legs, just brushing his cock.

Before they kissed again, he saw Marisa quickly scan the room once more. Apparently reassured, she let her eyes close and her kiss was hard and wet, full of aggressive passion. When their mouths parted, she smiled at him with her eyes — it was a look of recognition.

Marisa suddenly turned and stretched out her body, lying down on the sofa so that her head rested on Neil's lap. She nestled her cheek against his erection. She pushed her feet into the cushion and raised her legs, so that her dress slipped back and exposed even more of her thighs. Her knees swaying in the air, together, then apart.

"Ah, you want me so much," she said softly. "Don't you?"

"Yes, I do."

"Do you think that's a good idea?" Playful, teasing again.

"It's the only idea."

"But we can't rush. Desire is all anticipation, isn't it?"

"Not *all* anticipation."

Marisa laughed. "And fantasy, imagination."

"Not *all* fantasy and imagination," Neil insisted, grinning at her. "It involves action too, and fulfillment."

"But the right action."

"And what's the right action?"

"Oh, but that's where imagination and fantasy come in," Marisa said, as she continued to move the side of her face against the bulge in his pants. "I'm sorry, you're so sweet to me, but I don't want to rush. You'll be gone, you know, and I'll still be here. Remembering this."

"That's all right," Neil said, moved by her words.

"So many nights I spent in this room, on this couch, the television and the radio turned on. But I was alone and all I could do was imagine moments like this. What we would say, what we would do."

"Well, I'm here now."

"Better than any dream."

"I doubt that."

"No, really," Marisa protested. "I don't like boys. I imagined a man a little older, though not too much! A man considerate, intelligent, experienced, understanding. You're even more, you're a gift."

"So are you," Neil told her. His right hand was between her legs and he slid his finger beneath her wet panties, stroking her, gently pushing on and entering her. Marisa's body heaved and squirmed, her desire storming, barely contained. With his other hand he caressed her cheek again and rolled his fingertip along her upper lips — she took it, sucking hard. "And what did you imagine yourself saying?"

Marisa tugged on his finger, then opened her mouth as she looked up at Neil. "Two." He was confused for a second, but then understood, and he slipped his middle finger into her mouth too. Her eyes were fierce with need and desire. "Three." Three. "Four..." Four, her face taut, her teeth biting hard on his flesh. Eyes wide, staring up at him.

He continued stroking her swollen clitoris. She was so wet and hot, and he was enthralled by the way her body responded. Then she pushed his fingers away from her mouth and grabbed his head with both of her hands, her fingers clutching his hair, pulling his face down as she lifted herself to kiss him again, her tongue thrusting, her lips squeezing and pressing and pulling on his mouth and tongue, their chins now dripping with saliva. Marisa tasted so sweet and felt so wonderful. And how utterly glorious it was to break free of thought at last and plunge into the tornado.

⇒ 10 ⇐

Sound Chooses to Echo

They made love with gasping urgency and quickness on the scarred leather sofa. After only a few minutes of resting, Marisa slipped out of Neil's arms, sat up and straightened her dress. Her panties hung from one of her ankles. Neil reached down to remove them. He held them to his face for a second, smiling at her, and then put them in his pants pocket.

"Oh? What's that, your trophy?" Lightly mocking, playful.

"No. I just don't want you to put them back on."

"Ah, good. I'm not through with you, either."

"I'm glad to hear it."

Neil zipped his pants and buckled his belt. Marisa slid closer and leaned against him as he put his arm around her. Reckless, reckless — he knew that, but he didn't care. What really bothered him about their quick fuck was that it had been just that, a quick fuck.

"We both needed and wanted each other so much," Marisa said. "The first time had to be like that. Thunder and lightning."

"Yes." Neil gave a soft laugh. "The first time."

"And how do you know it won't be the same way the second time?" Marisa asked with a naughty grin. "And the third? We might make a lot of thunder and lightning, you know."

"That's great, if we do," he told her. "But I also want you in a bed, yours or mine, where we can take our time and really make love."

Marisa wriggled closer in his embrace, sighed happily and kissed his chin, running her hand along his leg. "So do I, and we will. But first we had to wait until they were in their rooms. And then — we couldn't wait a minute longer! But that's okay. Every time is good in its own way."

They sat together like that for a while longer, kissing, touching each other, all tenderness, affection and dreamy smiles. Neil loved the way she felt in his arms, the softness of her skin, the fragrance in her hair, the sweet spicy taste of her mouth.

Reckless, yes — but what the hell, if she got pregnant, he would marry Marisa and they would have a child. He would still write his books, it might even turn out to be a happy marriage and — Neil almost laughed aloud, it was such a startling and improbable thought. But what surprised him most was that it didn't scare him at all. His personal life had been drifting nowhere the last few years. Before that too, probably. Perhaps he had reached the point where he secretly hoped that some outside event would force a dramatic change that sent his life in a completely new and unexpected direction, and he would have no choice but to go along with it.

Things like that happened in opera all the time. Part of Neil's brain knew that in the cold light of day he would see it differently, rationally, and that he would probably want to drive away from Marisa and this house with no complications or lingering ties. But for now that part of his brain had no voice. He only wanted this wonderful erotic interlude to continue. Let the two of them see how much pleasure and deep comfort they could give to each other in a short period of time.

Marisa took his hand and they rose from the sofa. They ascended the narrow circular staircase. She smiled back over her shoulder at him when he put his hand on her hip. How he enjoyed the way her body felt as she moved, the smooth, elegant working of her perfect flesh and taut muscles. He slid his hands under Marisa's dress, caressing her thighs. She stopped near the top of the stairs, enjoying his touch, murmuring softly to herself. She turned and sat down on the top step, and opened her legs wide to him. She pulled the front of her dress back with one hand, while the other one partly covered her lush triangle of fine black hair.

Neil leaned forward, gripping the iron stair with his hands to brace himself. He ran his cheek down along the inside of her thigh — ah, it was so silky, warm and soft. Neil imagined he could feel an electric charge building as his skin moved over hers. His tongue probed between her fingers, but she wouldn't help him. Finally he touched and had a fleeting taste of her hot wet inner flesh, so tantalizing. He felt the little jump her body gave, and heard the brief but sharp intake of her breath. Marisa gently took his face in her hands and raised it. She was smiling so warmly and happily. Her hair fell over him as she pulled his face to her breasts and held him there for a moment. Then she slid her body back a little on the floor and stood up.

"My lover. Come on. Not here."

Neil took her hand again and followed her back into the corridor. It was very dark, except for a glimmer of light farther down on the right, where his room was. Marisa started to walk in that direction, but Neil looked to the left and saw the same faint blue glow he had seen earlier. He decided it was the perfect opportunity. He tightened his grip on her hand, and wouldn't move, so she turned around.

"Your room is this way," she told him. Her voice was low, almost a whisper. She tugged his hand.

"What's that blue light?"

He started walking toward the alcove. For some reason he expected Marisa to resist, but she didn't.

"Oh, that. You want to see? It's interesting."

They carefully went up the short flight of steps. There was barely room enough for both of them on the tiny landing. The alcove was virtually the same as before, with the shelf of votive candles still lit and the crude iron crucifix on the wall, but the bunk was empty — bare wood.

"What's this all about?"

"Remember, I told you that they think this house was once a religious retreat, something like that?"

"Oh, yes."

"Okay, so. My uncle thinks that this was a special place they used, where one priest or monk could shut himself in for a while to meditate or to pray." Marisa pointed to a couple of spots on the side walls. "You can see where there might have been hinges for a door. If you were inside, it would almost be like lying in a coffin, so it would help you to think about death, and God, and the life to come. Your movements would be completely restricted. You couldn't stand up or walk around, the way you could in your room. You have no window, no view. No distractions at all. There is nothing to do but lie there and think and pray. You see? Unusual, isn't it?"

Aside from the way she kept her voice down, she reminded Neil of so many bright young guides who explained things at the many historical sites he had visited.

"But why the candles now?"

"Oh." Marisa waved her hand dismissively. "The old women keep them lit all the time. They believe this story so strongly, they want to have it ready in case the soul of some holy man ever returns. Or to honor them all, like devotion candles in a church. Something like that."

"I see."

It made reasonable sense — except for the young man Neil had seen lying there in the bunk. The red sheet on him. His cold blue skin, the way it had appeared to react to his touch. But now Neil was wondering if perhaps he had imagined all of that. He couldn't mention it now.

"I used to think the candles were dangerous," Marisa went on. "But we depend on them in this house. We only have one generator, no connection to the national grid. But there's never been a fire so far. After a while, you get used to things and don't even think about them."

"Yes."

They backed out of the alcove, made their way down the dark steps and a few moments later were in Neil's room. There was no lock in the door but he felt a little better in some vague way when he pulled it shut and the old latch clicked loudly in place. He switched on the small lamp that was on the bedside table. It created a pocket of golden light around the bed but left the rest of the room in shadows.

Neil had his back half-turned to Marisa for a moment but he felt her presence close to him, like electricity in the air, a growing force of barely contained energy. She reached around him from behind and started tugging his shirt out, unbuttoning it, quickly unbuckling his belt, unzipping his pants again. Her hand slipped into his pocket for a second. Neil pulled his shirt and undershirt off, and immediately felt Marisa kissing his back, rubbing her face on his skin. Her mouth so wet and hot. His pants fell to the floor and he stepped out of them. He yanked his socks off, and was naked. He could feel her body give a slight shrug, he heard the rustle of her dress falling, and then he felt her bare breasts pressing against his back.

Marisa had removed her silk panties from his pocket and now she had them wrapped loosely around her hand as she took his cock and began to stroke it, sending waves of exquisite sensation through him. He reached behind with both hands, caressing her fanny, pulling her even more tightly to his body. She continued stroking him and he was very hard again. "Mmm," she murmured happily.

Neil turned and kissed her, his hands on her breasts and between her legs. He sat down on the bed, pulling her with him, but she stayed on her feet and straddled his legs. Marisa gently pushed him flat on his back, without breaking their long wet kiss, her body poised over his. She felt so wonderful and he loved the way her hair trailed across his skin. He moved farther onto the bed. She moved with him, letting her breasts hang so that her nipples just grazed along over his belly and chest. Then she swung one leg over him and lowered her hips, her body suddenly drawing him into her, seizing him in one swift, sure movement that made him gasp with pleasure.

She leaned forward, letting him kiss her breasts and suck her nipples as their lower bodies heaved violently together. Neil reached down to stroke her wet hard clitoris at the same time as their bodies were thrusting furiously, making the large bed rock and groan. Marisa's cries grew much louder, she no longer cared who might hear anything.

It was longer the second time, but not slower, and the pleasure they experienced was far more intense, ravishing both of them. Their bodies were drenched with sweat when they finally lay still together. Marisa kissed his neck, her lips moving weakly, the lightest of touches. Neil could only hold her in his arms.

He must have dozed off for a little while. Marisa was kissing him and telling him that she couldn't stay in his room all night, but that she would be back in the morning. Neil gave a little groan of unhappiness, but he smiled sleepily when he opened his eyes and saw her.

"Your face is red, all around your mouth," he said.

She grinned. "So is yours. And your lips are swollen up."

He smiled. "So are yours."

"Not just my lips!"

They laughed, kissed and hugged again, but then she left and the light went out and Neil immediately fell back into a deep happy sleep.

⸝⸙⸜

He was naked and cold, and he groped blindly for something to cover himself with. Then the voices entered his brain and stubbornly dragged him back to near-consciousness. Neil sat up slowly and opened his eyes. There was a little grey in the light that came through his open window. The voices were coming from somewhere outside. They were unintelligible, foreign, but surprisingly clear and sharp in the predawn silence.

Neil stood up and listened. He could still hear the voices, though they were a bit fainter now. He crossed the cold floor to the window. The air was very cool, but the cloudy fog — *il morbo* — had disappeared. It was still fairly dark outside but he could see things clearly enough.

⸝⸙⸜

In the distance, on one of the ridges about a hundred yards away, two men were walking. But no, there were three of them. They were moving in a direction away from the house. Their voices carried so well that it seemed to Neil almost like a ventriloquist's trick, as if they were standing on the ground just below his window. But he still couldn't understand anything they said. Their voices were gruff, angry, or so it sounded to Neil.

Then he realized dimly that two of the men were dragging and yanking the third one along. They appeared to hit and kick him, as necessary, to keep him moving. A struggle of some sort was in progress, but at such a distance it seemed merely curious to Neil, almost abstract. It went on like that for a little while longer, and then the three men disappeared beyond the downward curl of the winding ridge.

Neil stood there a moment longer, until he realized that he couldn't keep his eyes open and that he was nearly asleep on his feet. He was still so tired. He turned around and went back to bed, pulling the sheet and blankets up over him, clutching them tightly just beneath his chin.

Then he heard — somewhere in the distance, outside — a gunshot. But it was there and gone in an instant, and sleep had him.

⇒11⇐

The Second Day

A sound, a metal click too small and distant to stir him, nothing more than a transient pinprick on the otherwise blank expanse of Neil's sleep. But then something else, different and closer, a whisper of cloth, accompanied by a feeling of movement — his own. Marisa was in bed with him, he realized, suddenly aware of her warmth enveloping him, her radiant skin on his and her hair fanning across his belly as she took him in her mouth.

⇒⇐

"It's all right," she told him when she wriggled up and settled into his arms beneath the sheets. "My uncle is in the grotto. He says Mass there for the farmers every morning and then he visits with them afterward. He won't be back for a while."

"The grotto?"

"The *grotta rossa,* they call it. It's a cave in the mountain, it's on the other side of the hill out back. Over many years, they made it into a shrine to Our Lady. I'll show it to you later."

"What about your parents and grandparents?"

"Oh, they don't climb the stairs anymore. The only one who might walk in on us here is my uncle. He would be upset and hurt."

"And angry?"

"Well, maybe a little."

"What about the — the servants?"

Marisa sighed — unhappily, it seemed to Neil. "They will stay away until I instruct them to clean your room and make up your bed. When we go downstairs."

"Do they bother you?" He had spoken without thinking, so he quickly added, "Or am I just imagining that?"

She hesitated before admitting, "It is difficult."

Neil could tell that she didn't want to talk about it. They lay still for a few more moments, but then Marisa sat up in a sudden quick movement and smiled irrepressibly again. She was so beautiful, her black hair mussed, her magnificent breasts swaying slightly as she turned her body to face him, her eyes sparkling with life. She kissed his lips, his cheeks, his neck, his ears, a quick flurry of affectionate butterfly kisses. Neil felt a fresh wave of emotion surge through him, not merely lust or desire, but something more complicated and harder to define.

Suddenly he remembered that the men there were going to patch his radiator today, and then he would drive away to find the nearest town and a repair shop. An inn for the night. At least, that was the plan. But now Neil felt no urgency about leaving. He wondered if Marisa would ask him to stay for another night. Instead of letting him take a room in town. He could hire a taxi to drive him back here and pick him up again when his car was ready — which might take two or three days, if they had to order out to get the correct replacement radiator.

"Come on, now," she said, interrupting his thoughts. "We don't have *that* much time. I want to watch you shave."

⇒✦←

They ate breakfast on the patio. It was a mild sunny morning and the air was sweet. Neil had deliberately chosen to wait until mid-September for this trip, knowing that the hordes of the summer visitors would pretty much be gone by then. He and Marisa had fresh fruit, omelets and strong coffee. Neil felt awake again, though still a little tired.

They saw Father Anton returning to the house. He had a long brisk stride for a man of his apparent years. When he noticed Marisa and Neil on the patio, he veered off the path and stopped to say hello and exchange a few pleasantries with them, nodding and smiling. But it seemed as if his thoughts were on other matters, and he soon left them to go inside.

"It's much different today," Marisa said. "Better, easier, you know? Yesterday they didn't know you and they were kind of uncertain. But today, it's like you are part of the household."

Neil laughed. "Good. I was afraid that I was causing you problems with them. Not to mention the inconvenience."

"No," she scoffed. Neil loved the way emotion showed in even the smallest of her facial expressions. "It's good now, it's okay."

"Well, I'm glad."

"So, I was thinking. Since it's such a lovely morning, perhaps you would like to go for a walk. There are plenty of old paths and trails, and the countryside is quite nice around here."

He smiled at her. "I'd love to go for a walk with you."

"Ah. I was hoping you would say that." Marisa moistened her lips. "I want to touch you again, right now." Then she laughed happily at her own impatience. "Damn!"

A few minutes later, equipped with a small picnic basket and a large beach towel, they set off. When they had walked a little more than a hundred yards, Neil stopped for a moment and glanced back. Now he could see the side of the house where his room was, though he wasn't sure exactly which window was his. So they had to be on the same ridge where he had seen the three men early that morning.

"Is something wrong?" Marisa asked.

"No, not at all. I just realized that the way we're going is in the view I have from the window in my room."

"Yes."

"I woke up early this morning. Just for a moment."

"You did?"

"I heard voices out here and I saw some men on this path."

"I should have warned you," Marisa said. "Those people

make noise day and night. The old ones stay up late, drinking. Then the younger ones get up early to go about their work. They have no consideration. I'm very sorry, I hope they didn't disturb you."

"No, I fell right back to sleep."

"I'm glad."

"I thought I heard a gunshot."

"Yes, they hunt early in the morning," Marisa explained. "Sometimes they bring back a deer, or ducks and geese from the lake. They need the food. It's such a shame, you know."

"What is?"

"The land looks so beautiful — and it truly is. But it is *so* difficult to live on, almost impossible. All of the work that has to be done, it never ends, and it never seems like enough."

꒦꒦

They walked for nearly an hour. It was easy going, as the path never rose or descended too sharply. They stopped a few times to enjoy the views and to kiss. Marisa told him how she and her brother had explored all of the countryside for miles around as children, and she got Neil to tell her a little bit about the book he was working on. It was another Italian chronicle from Stendhal, he admitted. Marisa thought that was wonderful, but Neil knew the critics would probably tear into him for repeating himself. Oh well. For one thing, he didn't have a better idea.

The sun was almost directly overhead when Marisa led him off the faint path and through a brief stretch of high brush and small trees. A few minutes later they came out into a mossy clearing at the base of a rocky wall, an area not much larger than a good-sized living room. A clump of spindly birch trees provided some shade. A narrow stream of water flowed down the rocks and disappeared into the thick brush at the perimeter.

"We're here," Marisa announced. She spread the beach towel on the grass beneath the birches.

"Perfect," Neil said. He set the picnic basket down and went to the stream. He had worked up a light sweat, so he splashed his face with water. It was very cold and it felt great. A perfect place for a picnic.

Marisa was kneeling on the towel, sitting back on her heels. She had already removed her canvas shoes and tossed them onto the grass. She was wearing a peasant-style blouse and a loose skirt that came to mid-calf, but which was now bunched up just over her knees. Neil sat beside her, resting his back against the trunk of one of the birches.

"There's a bottle of wine in the basket," she said. "Some fresh bread, mortadella and cheese."

"Mmm."

She leaned forward on her hands, and she was like a big beautiful cat pressing against him. Still on her hands and knees, she positioned herself over his lap, and smiled up at him.

"Or would you like to play with me first?"

"*Mmmm...*"

Neil reached under, slipping his hand inside her blouse, caressing her breasts, teasing her nipples. His other hand moved beneath her skirt and up the back of her thigh — the sudden thrill of finding that she had no panties on, that her flesh was so hot and moist already. His finger moved into her easily and stroked and rubbed her. Marisa's eyes were closed, her mouth open, and she sighed and groaned with something more than pleasure, some longing and need so great that it seemed almost heartbreaking to Neil. Then she whipped her head back, hair flying, and her mouth tightened, her breath sharp and fast, grunting with ferocity. Neil stroked and caressed her until she sagged down on her forearms and rolled her face in his crotch. Feeling how hard he was, she lithely swung her body around so that her backside faced him. She pulled her skirt up over her hips.

"Please, now..."

Neil quickly pulled his pants down, knelt behind her, took hold of her and then thrust into her. Such dizzying pleasure, laced with a passing spasm of sharp pain. Marisa cried out urgently.

"Harder, harder..."

She swung her head back and forth in the air again. Neil grabbed her long hair in one hand, carefully pulling it taut. She tilted her head back, and then he could see the wild smile, the roaring look on her face — her eyes open and fiery, urging him, challenging him.

"Harder harder...make me feel you...more...MORE!"

Her cries were so loud now. Sweat stung Neil's eyes as he slammed into her again and again, and Marisa went down, her face pressed against the towel, her arms splayed out, hands clutching the cotton, her eyes closed again now, and he forced her hips down to the ground too, his body pressed on hers as he came, his face buried in her hair.

⋙✄⋘

"My lover..."

"*My* lover," Neil said, stroking her face.

"Ah." Marisa put on an impish smile. "I think maybe you better not say anything more right now."

"Will you come to Rome? At least to visit?"

Her eyes widened in mock-suprise. "See what I mean?" She pressed her finger to his lips. "*Sssh*. Who knows?" She kissed him again.

>€

It was the middle of the afternoon by the time Neil and Marisa arrived back at the house. They found two men pondering Neil's radiator, which was on a large sheet of plastic on the ground. They were daubing it with a tar-like substance. Much of the front end of the car had been dismantled, with loose parts scattered all around. One of the men launched into a long and detailed explanation — to Marisa — that involved hand-waving and pointing to various tricky places on the radiator. Neil didn't understand a word they spoke but it was quite obvious that he wasn't going anywhere that day. He didn't mind, in fact he felt a distinct sense of relief.

"It's difficult," Marisa explained. "There's so much corrosion, so many spots for them to patch up."

Neil nodded. "I can see how bad it is."

"Maybe by tomorrow?"

"Okay."

"Anyhow, if they can't get it working again, my brother will be home by the end of the week."

"Even better."

Marisa tried not to smile. "It's a good thing they don't speak English. You're very naughty!"

Neil smiled at her. "I'm trying."

12

The Last Night

Neil was exhausted by the long walk and their intense lovemaking, so he was glad when Marisa suggested another late afternoon siesta. She led him back to his room, promising to return for him later. He was also grateful to hear that they were excused from dinner with the family that night. He had no desire to find out what might be on the menu this time. Though in all fairness to them, it was their house and he was the intruder, and Marisa's family probably felt just as uncomfortable as Neil had.

But what a bizarre, sad household it was. What would he make of all this without Marisa? As Neil stretched out on the bed and nestled his head in the soft pillow, he realized that since he had arrived there yesterday he'd had almost no time to think about anything. The one instance when he had a few moments alone, Neil had heard the unusual metal scraping sound and he had discovered that peculiar alcove, which may or may not have had the body of a young man in it. Otherwise, Marisa was with him, occupying his thoughts and attention, or else he was too tired and sleepy to think.

Marisa was wonderful. He loved the way she made him respond naturally, instinctively — without the need for thought or analysis. She had such a gift and an appetite for living, it seemed to him. It was a terrible thing that she was stuck here, so unfair and unnatural. Her own personal life was indefinitely on hold.

Neil had to find the right way to speak to Marisa about it, to make her see that she had to do something — for her own sake. She could at least try to get away for a few days every month, to Rome, anywhere. Just to be among other people, to stroll about a city, eat in a restaurant, see a movie...

He was about ten years older than Marisa was, but that didn't seem to matter to her and it certainly didn't to him. Maybe a real relationship would never work out, but Neil had a strong sense that he could not just drive away and let go without even trying.

He had to leave...but he had to see her again...

...wanted her...

His eyes closed.

"Do we have to wait for everybody to go to bed again tonight?" Neil asked, smiling at her.

"You're so naughty, I love it," Marisa said, laughing. "No, we don't. I have a special place I want to show you."

They were finishing a light meal in the billards room. Some vacuous Euro-techno music droned on the radio in the background. Marisa looked very pretty, very girlish in a dark blue-green plaid skirt that almost reached her knees and a white short-sleeved blouse that was somehow even sexier to Neil because it was buttoned all the way to the top. She wore several thin silver bracelets on her wrists. She had braided some of the hair on the sides of her head and tied it with beaded blue bands.

"I had to tidy it up while you were sleeping," Marisa continued. "I had not been down there for years."

"*Down* there?"

"Yes." She pointed to the floor. "There's a huge cellar beneath this house. It's full of things my family brought with them after the war and have never used since. I don't know what we'll do with it."

"But they were lucky they could take anything at all with them," Neil said. "By the end of the war tens, probably hundreds of thousands of people had nothing more than the clothes on their backs."

"Yes, I suppose. Anyhow, when we were children, Hugo and I had our own little clubhouse down there. It's buried in the middle of everything. It was a good place to hang out on rainy days. Later, I used to like to go there alone, to read or just to think. You know?"

"Sure." Neil nodded. "The childhood retreat, the adolescent haven. We all had private hideouts like that."

Marisa laughed. "Hideouts — yes, that's the word."

She took his hand. Neil thought that they were heading toward the front of the house, but as usual there were so many turns and passages that it was impossible for him to keep a sense of direction. They finally arrived at the door that led to the cellar. As soon as Marisa opened it, Neil heard the sound of an electric generator. She flicked a switch and some lights went on below. The narrow stone stairs descended along an interior wall that was made of rock and mortar, and were open on the other side.

"Watch your step," she warned him.

Neil nodded. The air was cool and damp, but he could tell from his first few breaths that it probably wouldn't bother him. The unbroken flight of stairs was steep and long — it was more like two normal floor levels down to the bottom, Neil estimated.

They had not quite gone halfway when Marisa stopped and turned to him. She pointed out across the expanse of the cellar now visible on the one side. Single light bulbs dangled from cables here and there, providing some illumination, though much of the place was cast in shadows.

"Look at it," she said, sounding exasperated.

"I see what you mean."

The place was a vast warren of storage areas, shelves and platforms, all of them full of boxes, cartons and trunks. One area contained metal racks jammed with clothing on hangers — coats, dresses, suits, shirts. Another part was given over to larger items that were covered with tarp, unusual shapes, some kind of equipment or tools.

"This is only half of it," Marisa told him. "It's the same on the other side of this wall."

"Wow, it looks like they brought everything with them."

"Oh, no, not at all. You'll never guess."

"Guess what?"

"What my families did, before they came here. Both of the families, my mother's and my father's. They worked together."

"Weren't they farmers, like here?"

Marisa laughed. "No!"

"Then I have no idea."

"Don't worry, I'll show you."

At the bottom of the stairs she led him around the wall into the other half of the cellar. At first it looked like more of the same, a maze of aisles and clogged passages through a sea of accumulated possessions. It was hard to see much because the light bulbs were widely scattered and dim, but Neil noticed a few unusual items — large rolls of canvas, for instance, a collection of grotesque puppets, some faded banners mounted on poles.

"Yes?" Marisa prompted.

"Still no idea," Neil said. "Unless they ran a circus."

"Ah, you're getting warm."

"Really?"

"Yes, they had a travelling show, not really a circus. In good weather they would go from town to town, the larger villages, throughout the entire region. They had a puppet show, they staged little plays, usually stories from the New Testament, things like that."

"Are you part gipsy?" Neil asked jokingly.

"No way," Marisa exclaimed. Neil found her sudden use of such an American expression endearing. "Those people, they call themselves Roma now, but they were trouble wherever they went. They made it very hard for families like mine. Nobody liked or trusted them. Gipsies, I mean."

"Nobody likes the gipsies," Neil echoed, trying to keep the sarcasm out of his voice. "Even today, even in America."

"Of course. But never mind them. I want to show you something that my great-grandfather did. I'm not sure if he started it. Probably not. But he was a master craftsman. Now forgotten, unknown."

The sadness in her voice struck Neil. They had come to a long table that was covered with wooden boxes, each one about the size of a medicine cabinet. Marisa went to one directly beneath a light bulb and lifted the lid. Neil stood close beside her. She carefully peeled back a sheet of something that looked like parchment or vellum, revealing a mask of a human face. The detail was remarkable.

"It's wax," Marisa said. "Look how fine the work is."

She slipped her fingers under the mask and lifted it — and Neil could see that it was almost paper-thin and translucent.

"Go ahead, it's okay," she told him. "You can touch it."

Neil took one edge of the mask between his fingers, rolling them over the filmy wax. It felt strong enough not to tear easily, but also very soft and supple. It had a slight oily slickness.

"What did they do with them?" he asked.

"They wore them in the plays they put on. And I think maybe they showed them, like an art exhibition — you know? One of the banners they used translates as 'The

House of Masks.' You see, the trick is, he cast them from
real people, and then he used the casts to make these masks.
He had some formula he developed to make the wax
like this."

"It's beautiful," Neil said. "But doesn't your grandfather
know how it's done? You could do something with this,
you know."

"Yes, he must know, but he won't say. He won't talk
about it at all anymore." Marisa shook her head sadly. "I'm
so afraid it will all be lost, because Hugo and I just don't
know what to do about it."

"Your father?"

"Same thing. He probably knows, but if I try to bring
up the subject, he switches off. Like *that*," she said snapping
her fingers.

Neil looked down the length of the table — tables, as he
realized there were three of them lined up end to end. "All
of these boxes —"

"Yes, each one contains several masks."

"Do you take care of them?"

"Ah, good question, my lover." Marisa was still holding
the mask in her hands. "Hugo and I are the only ones who
have ever even looked at them in the last fifty years, yet this
is how they are. The temperature and moisture in the air
here must be just right. And wax is a remarkable substance
in the right conditions. It doesn't change."

"Fifty years. God. It does feel a little oily."

"Yes," she agreed quickly. "I think they were condi-
tioned or rubbed with some kind of plant oil to help preserve them this way."

Marisa laid the mask back in the wooden box and arranged the cover sheet over it. She closed the lid and fastened the hasp, and then looked up at Neil with a quizzical expression on her face.

"I was a history student at university," she said. "You write about history. But do you have any idea how much history is here, in this cellar? I mean real history? What they saw, what they lived through?"

"Look at them," Neil said, his voice suddenly loud. "Your parents and grandparents, all still alive. All that history. You should get them to tell you about it, everything they can remember. Write it down, or better yet, get it on tape. Marisa, you can still do this."

"Ah, they won't talk," she said with a shrug of resignation. Then she smiled again. "Come on, we're not there yet."

⇒ 13 ⇐

Between Sleep and Death

They only had to go a short distance farther. Neil noticed that they were nearing one of the outer walls of the cellar. The dark expanse of rock loomed above them, and it was laced with alkaline encrustations, which in certain places appeared to glow with a faint greenish phosphorescence. Neil could only wonder at the age of the house and the labor that must have been involved in the construction of the cellar walls alone.

They stepped out of the shadows and stood beneath a light bulb in a small clear area in front of what looked exactly like a miniature house. There were two wooden steps up to the narrow door, on either side of which was a tiny square window. The house was only about eight feet wide and not quite twice that in length. The back end stood flush against the cellar wall.

"This was one of the wagons they used a hundred years ago," Marisa told him. "Probably long before that too. Who knows."

"A wagon?" Neil was surprised, but then he could see that it made perfect sense. He saw where the wheels had been, and that the front steps, as he first thought of them, were in fact where the driver would sit when they were travelling. The house was painted in blue and gold and the curved roof was red — at one time it must have been very bright and eye-catching, Neil thought. There *was* even a small but ornate overhang above the door. It was a relic of history, as Marisa had said. Neil could easily imagine a train of these wagons making their way over the unpaved roads of a Europe that had long since vanished.

Marisa seemed to sense what he was thinking, and said nothing for a moment. Neil was still taking in details, like the small wooden box fastened beneath each window, to hold a flower pot.

"It's astonishing how much they brought over," he remarked. "I don't know how they ever managed it."

"They were lucky to get out," Marisa replied. "They told me it was the end of the war, but I believe they must have started long before that. They probably began sending the wagons overland at least a year before. And how they managed it, that's simple. They bribed their way."

"Oh, of course."

"Gold, jewels."

"You must try to get them to tell you more," Neil said. "The details, what it was like every day and night for them. Real history is not just in the big events, but in what ordinary people lived through. You should do it, not necessarily because you want to do anything with it, like turn it into a book, but for yourself. For you to know."

"Yes, I should." Marisa turned to a small table nearby. She took a wooden match and lit a candle. No electricity inside.

Neil followed her up the two steps. She opened the door and went in. She put the candle on a shelf and then lit a couple of others that were already placed around the room. Neil had to duck his head to get inside. One of the candles must have been scented because he immediately noticed the fragrance of lavender in the air.

"Close the door," she said, smiling broadly. "Take your shoes and socks off, make yourself at home."

Neil slid the bolt in place — this door actually locked. Marisa pulled the tiny curtains across the windows.

The floor inside the wagon was covered with an old oriental carpet. There was almost no furniture, just a small low table surrounded by cushions and pillows — dozens of them, in various sizes and colors. On the table was a bottle of wine, already opened, with the cork sitting loosely in place, two glasses and a platter of antipasto covered with a glass lid. There was even a shallow bowl of water filled with floating purple flowers.

It all reminded Neil of the way that some guys he had known would prepare their apartment when they were having a girl in for the evening. But here — in this dismal pit of a cellar beneath an old house out in the middle of nowhere. His poor Marisa. It was touching, but ultimately so sad. And yet, Neil was happy to be there with her.

"It's great," he said. "You must have done a lot of work."

Marisa gestured as if she were wiping her brow, and then stifling a big yawn. "You had a nap today. I didn't!"

"Ah, baby. Let me pour you some wine."

"That sounds very good."

They stretched out together on the pillows, half-sitting, resting back, their bodies touching, Neil's arm around her shoulder. He unbuttoned her blouse enough so that he could slip his hand inside and hold her breast.

"Mmmm."

They relaxed like that in silence for a few moments. Neil was still thinking of how to phrase what he wanted to say to her when Marisa began to speak, her voice quiet, reflective.

"Do you believe in life after death?"

"What?"

"I mean, my family does. They're devout Catholics — more Catholic than the Pope, my uncle always says — and they believe in life eternal through Christ. I was just wondering, do you?"

"I was raised a Catholic too."

"And?"

Neil smiled, admiring the way she wouldn't let him dodge that one. "No, I stopped believing that a long time ago."

"Are you sure?"

"Well, yes. But you never really know. Until."

"Ah."

"Do you?"

"Do I what? Believe that?"

"Yes."

"Not the same way," Marisa said. "But I think maybe we do live on in another form. You know what I think it is like? Have you ever been just a little bit awake, but still almost totally asleep? You have an awareness, but you feel like you have no body. You feel like you're floating in a vast ocean, but it's not water, it's not air. There's no color, nothing to see. You are just *being* there, and *there* is nowhere. You're alone. All alone. You don't see anything, you can't smell or hear anything. Nothing touches you, because you have no body. There is nothing you need, nothing you want. You don't even have any thoughts. No memories to please or hurt you. And yet you do have some kind of awareness. I don't know what other word to use. Awareness. Like, you know you exist. And you understand. Yourself. Everything. Your awareness encompasses all your memories and experiences, and more, but it isn't limited just to them, it never calls them up as scenes or words. Do you know what I mean? Your awareness is complete. In this — nothing. And the amazing part of it is, all you have is this awareness, but you are *content*. You can be this way forever, regardless of whether you're lying in a grave or your ashes were scattered to the wind. You still *are*, and you're content."

"What would be the point?" Neil asked after a moment.

Marisa laughed, dispelling the solemn mood. "We used to talk like this at the university, late at night. Student talk."

"That's all right. But I have no answers."

"Of course, nobody does. I was just talking, imagining out loud," she said apologetically. "I've gone so long without anyone to talk to."

"You have to get away from here."

Marisa propped herself up on one elbow. "Impossible."

"No, it's very possible."

"Never mind that now. Let's be bad. Let's fuck."

Neil smiled. He started to pull her to him to kiss her, but she slipped out of his arms, giggling. She crawled across his body and reached behind a large pillow for something on the floor. Neil ran his hand up her leg, stroking her thigh, his fingers teasing. She murmured happily and wiggled her feet in the air, but rolled off his lap and sat up.

"Here."

She was holding a wooden box. It was just like the ones on the tables outside that contained the masks.

⇒ 14 ⇐

figures in Wax

"I want to try something with you," she said, her eyes shining with promise and anticipation. "If you don't like it, that's okay."

"What is it?"

"You'll see!"

Marisa put the box down on a pillow beside them. She pulled her skirt up and swung her body so that her legs straddled his and she was facing him, half-sitting on his lap. She loved this position and so did he. Neil put his hands on her bare thighs for a moment, and then finished unbuttoning her blouse while she did the same with his shirt. She was wearing a half-bra that unhooked in front. She looked wildly sexy with her clothes hanging open like that. She kissed him teasingly, her mouth wet, her tongue dancing and licking lightly, but she pulled back every few seconds. She had his slacks open now. Her touch was tantalizing — again and again Marisa's fingers brushed slowly along his cock, and then moved away. Neil cupped her breasts in his hands, bending forward to suck and tug her hard nipples between his lips, teasing them with his tongue. Although they were still only playing — their eyes were open, smiling, widening, urging each other on — he was already completely caught up again in the long beautiful whirl of desire and arousal. But then she put her hands on his face, holding him for a moment.

"These are the most remarkable masks my great-grandfather ever made," Marisa said as she reached to open the box — Neil had almost forgotten about that box. "I put one of them on once. It was incredible. Now I want to do it again, with you. I want you to see what it's like."

It sounded kind of silly, but Neil shrugged. "Okay."

"Ah, my lover, I love your romantic soul."

"And I love yours."

Marisa carefully lifted a mask from the box. It was clearly unlike the one Neil had seen before, on the table outside the wagon. This mask hung in the air almost like some clingy, nearly transparent fabric. Marisa spread her fingers and the facial features in the mask became apparent. The eyes, nose and mouth were open, though little more than slits.

"Me first," she said.

Neil gave a short laugh. "Fine."

She tilted her head back slightly, closed her eyes and shook her hair away from her face. Then she raised the mask and let it fall gently into place on her skin. She blinked her eyes a couple of times and moved her lips open and shut, twisting them once or twice. She smiled at him. She looked almost the same, but different in some subtle way Neil couldn't immediately define. Younger? Her strong features even stronger, more dramatic? They wore these masks in Bible stories, he reminded himself. Like masks or makeup for opera singers, they were probably intended to heighten and emphasize certain basic character features or flaws for the benefit of an audience. With Marisa, he thought, the mask made her look even younger than she was, like a fierce, precocious teenager. Her expression seemed to convey even more forcefully the great depths of her powerful sensual nature.

Neil touched her cheek, and was astonished. It still felt like her skin, warm, soft and silky smooth, and yet he thought he could also feel some added vibrancy, like a wild hidden current that suddenly finds its outlet. The mask fit the contours of her face amazingly well.

Marisa picked up another mask and held it open for him. But before Neil would put it on he had to test it and make sure that it wouldn't trigger an asthmatic reaction. He thought of wax as essentially odorless, but there was no way of knowing what chemicals might have been used in the preparation of the mask. He put his face close to it, and inhaled. Again, closer and more deeply the second time. Yes, there was something, but it was not the kind of chemicals Neil had feared. Mint? Anyhow, it was all right.

"It's hard to believe this is actually wax," he said. "It's so fine and supple. It's almost as thin as plastic wrap, but it has body."

"I know, but there are dozens of different kinds of wax in nature and they are very adaptable. Are you ready?"

"Sure."

Marisa helped him position the mask over his face. It seemed to float in the air for a second before settling down on his skin. Neil blinked his eyes a couple of times — he could feel the mask close around them, but there was no impairment or discomfort. He touched his eyebrows — he could feel the mask over them, yet at the same time Neil had the illusion of touching the hair itself. It was remarkable, just as Marisa had said.

Now he caught the essence of the mask in his nostrils and mouth. He thought he detected a sweetness, like honey. As in honey, bees and beeswax? That made sense. Something else, stronger than any of the mints. It had to be wintergreen, Neil thought. He could almost feel it shooting light into dormant and dark corners of his brain, it was so invigorating and stimulating.

Marisa ran her fingertips over his face, smoothing down a few loose parts of the mask. Her touch was exquisite, setting off tiny flares of pleasure in his skin. She smiled when she saw him react.

"Are you all right?"

"Fine," he replied.

"Are you sure?"

"Oh yes," he said emphatically.

Her face was very close to his. She touched his lips,

licking along them slowly — Neil trembled with sudden delight. Her breath seemed to enter his pores. It was soft and sweet, as delicious as the air on a beautiful summer night.

"You don't want to take it off?"

"No...not yet...and don't stop what you're doing..."

"I haven't even started." Marisa took his lower lip between her teeth and bit until it began to hurt him, and then she pressed it tenderly between her wet lips for just a moment before releasing him. Anticipation...

She kissed him hard and pushed him back on the pillows, her tongue thrusting into his mouth, and it felt like their faces were merging, possessed of each other in brilliant consuming flames of desire. Energy and hunger for her roared through him, every nerve in his body seemed to pulse and buzz anxiously. He rolled Marisa over onto her back and then broke their kiss as he pulled her blouse wide open to get at her breasts, rubbing them with his face — it felt like a wonderful shower of sensation in their skin, a cascading rain of pleasure. She wrapped her legs around him and dug her heels into his backside, pulling him into her as she cried out, urging him on, her voice loud, becoming a long staccato shriek that filled the little room.

⇒✦⇐

Their bodies glowed like hot coals. Everything seemed so vivid to Neil, the infinite beauty of the way their bodies fit together and how they felt in the perfect peace and silence afterward. But Marisa could not wait more than a couple of minutes. He was still in her, his face on her shoulder. She gently turned his head a little so that he could see her eyes.

"My lover."

"Mmm..."

"Now, tell me."

"Tell you what?"

"Wasn't that the best fuck you ever had?"

She put her hand over her mouth, as if she'd said something naughty, but it didn't hide her impish smile.

Neil laughed. "By far," he answered truthfully.

"But, no." Marisa shook her head contrarily. "I don't think so. The *next* one is."

She slid out from under him and sat up. He saw her hand reach back to the wooden box. Too soon, he was thinking in a haze. I'm thirty-five, not nineteen. She had another mask in her hand. She reached between his legs and began to stroke him with it.

She was right.

><

Neil had no idea what time it was when he awoke, but it was so quiet that he could hear one of the candles guttering. He felt cold. Then he looked around and discovered that he was alone in the wagon. His face felt tight and somehow unnatural — the mask, he remembered. He pulled at it and he could feel it with his fingertips, but he couldn't get ahold of it.

"Marisa?"

Perhaps there was a back room — but no, as soon as he looked he saw that there was a rear door, but no other compartment in the wagon. He was alone. Neil stood up, still plucking at the mask. He thought he could feel the edge of it, but his attempts to push or roll it back failed.

"Marisa!"

It was a trick, just the kind of thing she would do. To tease him. He could imagine her laughing, then acting sheepish, the naughty girl. He would undoubtedly forgive her, but right now he felt angry. It seemed impossible to get the mask off his face. She would know how to do it, some simple method, or perhaps you had to use a liquid solution of some sort.

He tried the door, but the bolt wouldn't move — it was rusted in place and didn't budge. Neil kicked at it repeatedly, until he was out of breath. He stood in the little room, gasping, trying to think.

The mask felt hot and very tight on his face — it seemed almost to be alive in itself. On him. He tore at it in a rage, trying to dig his nails into it and rip it away. Neil felt the sudden raking pain in his cheek. It was as if he were scratching deeply into his own skin, but his fingers slid uselessly along the smooth, unyielding surface of the mask.

⇒ 15 ⇐

By the River Sava

The wagon rocked. The rear door splintered, tore loose
and crashed to the floor. Neil was stunned. He had no idea
at all what was happening. He could only stand there and
gape at the sudden terrifying eruption of noise and violence.
Three men in dark uniforms rushed through the open
doorway. Two of them carried pistols, while the third had
a short, wide-blade sword. Their boots thudded heavily.
The men shouted angrily at him in a language he didn't

understand, though it did sound familiar to him, probably the language of Marisa's parents.

Neil had no doubt that they meant to kill him. Fear paralyzed him, but he opened his mouth to protest. The first man hit him hard across the side of the head with the butt of his gun. Neil was dazed and fell against one of the side walls. Before he could recover his balance, two of the men set on him. They pummeled him about the head and face with their weapons. Neil held his arms up in an attempt to ward off the flurry of blows. The men kicked at him, yanked him across the room, and flung him out the door.

Neil flew through the air and landed painfully on hard rough ground. He was outdoors. He moaned and couldn't move for a minute. His head was pounding and he could taste his own blood in his mouth, but — absurdly — his mind still tried to calculate: the rear of the wagon had been backed up against the cellar wall, so there had to be an entrance to the outside there that he had not been able to see, one large enough to admit wagons, and —

But the immediate reality overwhelmed attempts at thought. Someone kicked him again. Neil jumped to his feet. The night air was full of shouting voices, loud cries and sporadic gunfire. He saw that he was in a group of a dozen or so men. They were in an open area, a kind of courtyard bordered by wooden barn-like buildings — none of which resembled Marisa's house. The area was illuminated by a few street lamps mounted on wooden poles and by some rooftop spotlights that slowly swept through the darkness. The armed men in uniform — were they the police, or soldiers? — quickly herded Neil's group across the square. He saw a similar group of men ahead of them — but then it vanished into an alley between two buildings.

One of the men near Neil suddenly stumbled and lunged a couple of paces out of the group, trying to regain his balance. A guard stepped toward him and almost casually stuck his knife out, into the man's throat. The man fell, gagging, spurting blood and clutching uselessly at his throat. The guard stood over him and shot him once in the back of the neck. The man's thick hair fanned like wheat in a sudden gust of wind. He fell flat on his face and didn't move again.

Neil's eyes frantically scanned the area as he ran with the others. He saw numerous bodies on the ground. Off to one side a man struggled with a guard, but two other guards hastened to converge on him, and he fell beneath a torrent of knife thrusts. Then the first guard stomped on the man's throat several times with his boot.

The narrow alley was directly in front of them. The guards smoothly funneled Neil's group into the dark passage with more angry shouts and kicks, and by jabbing at them with their knives. At the other end, twenty or thirty yards ahead, another cluster of guards took control of the group and marched them across a much larger piece of open ground — though it was not actually open, Neil realized, when he saw the barbed wire fencing. The area was lit by more spotlights and several scattered bonfires. A three-quarters moon emerged from behind some clouds and added to the garish lighting. He saw a wide ribbon of water in the distance. For an instant he could even see that it was moving — a river.

But nearer, all around, were the bodies of dead men.

Neil and the others were made to lie face down on the ground. Here every guard — and there were many more of them — carried both a pistol and either a sword or a club. One man raised his head to look around and a guard swiftly stepped in and kicked the man in the face. Neil was careful, moving his head only fractions of an inch at a time to see as much as he could of what was happening. A kind of low-level pandemonium reigned. No one seemed to be in charge, but it was obviously a killing ground.

Suddenly Neil had to restrain himself to keep from shouting because he recognized someone. He had a clear view as two guards were leading a man past Neil's group — it was the same man who had brought the water for the radiator of Neil's car the other day. Perhaps he ought to shout to the man, even if it brought some punishment. The man would recognize him, perhaps he would say something, tell someone — but then the man and the two guards disappeared from sight.

Now someone from Neil's group was hauled to his feet and brought a few yards ahead, where he was engaged in an apparently heated conversation with three of the guards. He was a young man, in his twenties. He repeatedly shook his head at whatever the guards were saying. Then a priest arrived on the scene. Neil again wanted to shout — an instinct learned in childhood, that you can always turn to a priest for help. But it was so startling to see one in all of this madness — what was he doing there? The priest spoke briefly with him, and then walked briskly away.

The guards immediately began to stab and hack at the young man with their swords, slicing off pieces of his shirt and chunks of flesh from his back and arms. One of them pushed a knife into the man's midsection and slashed downward, spilling organs in a huge gush of blood. His scream was cut off when another guard swung a club and smashed it into his mouth, sending teeth and more blood through the air. The helpless man was still twitching wildly and gasping raggedly as they dragged him out of sight. Neil turned his face downward and away.

What lunacy was this? He knew from the sharp grit pressing against his face on the ground that it was no dream, no hallucination, and yet his mind did not seem to be functioning clearly. He'd been in the wagon with Marisa, they had put on the masks and made love — twice, three times? But then Neil realized he still had the mask on his face, he could feel it there again, tight on his skin, the taste of honey and wintergreen. He reached to touch it, to pull at it — a club blow on the side of the head rocked him.

A few moments later, when he opened his eyes, he saw a priest again, but a different kind of priest. Eastern or Greek Orthodox, perhaps. He was fifty or sixty feet away, he had an unusual hat or vestment on his head, and his beard was full and squarish. The guards were talking to him in an animated fashion but the priest simply ignored them. He looked about forty years old. He didn't move or acknowledge the guards in any way. His eyes remained locked onto an invisible point no one else could see — the priest appeared to be focused entirely on his own thoughts.

One of the guards suddenly grabbed the priest's beard and hacked at it with a knife. Patches of wet redness opened on his face, but he sat still and had the same distant, stoic look in his eyes. The others were laughing along with this or else silently watching with smirks of mild amusement. After the guard had slashed off several chunks of hair and skin, he stepped behind the priest, knocked the headpiece off, pulled the man's head back by the hair and slowly dug a knife through his throat. The priest's eyelids fluttered open and closed a few times, then remained half open. After a few moments, when the eruption of blood slowed, the guard dug in harder with the knife. He couldn't manage it and became increasingly angry. Then one of the other guards came up with a hatchet and attacked the back of the neck, where the spinal cord and the brain meet, and after a few swings — flesh in the air like chips of wood — the priest's head was finally cut loose. The guard shouted happily and held it in the air, while the body sagged and toppled to the ground.

Think. Try to think. If I could only think —

He was aware of others in the group being moved, lifted up and taken somewhere beyond his line of vision, one at a time. Neil thought again of the man who was supposed to fix his car. Was he a prisoner too, like the rest of them? Or was he with —

A shout and a painful kick in the ribs told Neil it was his turn. He got up, feeling certain that he was about to experience his own death. He had no idea why, and there was apparently nothing he could do about it but go along with it. As two guards pushed and steered him roughly, Neil wondered if he could somehow break free, run and dodge their bullets. Run toward the river and escape? But he had already seen others try that and he knew that it would be a pointless gesture.

They passed a small group of guards tormenting a man who staggered blindly in circles. His hands were tied behind his back. The guards had put a strange wooden box with bolts and leather straps over the man's head. It seemed to fit tightly and was probably smothering him. They cut his belt and tugged his pants down, and then jabbed their knives at his genitals. The man jumped and twisted, trying vainly to avoid each cutting thrust, but he couldn't see anything. His cries were muffled by the wooden box. The last glimpse Neil had — one guard was furiously slashing off a thick strip of flesh from the doomed man's pale buttocks.

A short distance farther, they came to a large cluster of guards. The circle parted to admit them and Neil was held tightly by two guards. He was allowed to watch a teenage boy, who seemed to be begging for his life. Neil couldn't see the people the youth was addressing, but he saw the desperation in his face. The boy made the sign of the cross, bowed his head, looked up hopefully and invoked the name of Jesus Christ, and then repeated the same sequence of gestures and words. One of the guards nudged Neil and nodded, as if to say that this was what he would be expected to do. Neil assumed that it meant he was to make his peace with God before he died.

The crowd tightened and necks craned, and Neil couldn't see what was happening. Everyone was quiet, but one voiced intoned softly. Then the guards began to laugh and clap, and suddenly Neil saw the boy's face again. He stood up, smiling cautiously. For just a moment, an air of bizarre gaiety seemed to prevail. But then two guards seized the boy. A third one held him tightly by the hair, pulling his head back. A fourth stepped forward to hit the boy's face with a metal tool — pliers. As soon as the boy's mouth opened, the guard clamped the pliers on his tongue. The boy struggled and tried to close his mouth, but couldn't do anything. With his other hand, the guard carefully slipped the blade of a knife between the boy's teeth. One of the other guards kicked the boy in the groin to make things easier. The boy's mouth opened wider involuntarily and he gave a strangled cry. The guard quickly flicked his wrist and came away with the boy's tongue in the pliers. This brought an enthusiastic burst of applause and more cheers. The boy was dragged off, his mouth foaming red, and a few seconds later Neil heard a gunshot.

Then he was hauled around to the center of the circle and flung to the ground. In front of him, torn and muddied, covered with gobs of spit, was a book in some unrecognizable language. Neil tried to think. The script was Cyrillic, he knew that much. When he looked up, Neil saw Marisa's uncle, Father Anton, smiling down at him.

The priest showed no sign of recognition. He was speaking softly and calmly, his hands making small gestures in the air, as if explaining things. When he finished, he pointed down to the book on the ground. Father Anton gazed at him with implacable indifference. Neil sensed that he had just a few seconds to reach some decision, and he understood. Marisa told him that her uncle was doing a study on conversions. That's what this was, a conversion. He was expected to renounce the book on the ground, whatever it was, and to proclaim his faith and allegiance to the one true Church.

The teenage boy — so that was what he had done. He had given in, he had renounced his faith, spit on the book and sworn himself to Christ. That's why they had cheered. But then they had cut out his tongue. Why? Probably so that he would not be able to recant — in the brief moment when he saw the pistol being aimed at him.

"Padre Anton," Neil said anxiously. *"Padre Panic. Sono gia un cattolico."*

The priest registered mild surprise, perhaps at both the words and the use of the Italian language. Neil could sense a flutter of curiosity among the guards around him, who fell silent and edged closer.

"Sono gia un cattolico," he repeated firmly. *"Dove e Marisa?* She will tell you. I'm a friend of hers." That involuntary lapse into English only seemed to confuse the priest. *"Devo vedere Marisa! Dove e Marisa, il mio amico, il mio caro?"*

Father Anton laughed as if he had just heard something ridiculous. A young man elbowed his way through the circle of guards and stood over Neil, who recognized him immediately — here was the person he had seen lying in the alcove bunk, in the house. Now this handsome young man glared at Neil. He wore a black leather coat over a grey suit. He swung his arm back. Neil saw the blackjack coming all the way.

Wow, a genuine leather blackjack — he thought, before it hit his head and sent his brain reeling into darkness — imagine that.

16

Stara Gradiska

The moon danced wildly in the sky above him. He was still there. He could hear the shouts, the screams, the random gunshots. His head rolled painfully on bare boards. A dark building floated by, then a tower. He was moving — he was being taken somewhere. When Neil finally got his eyes to focus he saw that he was lying in the back of a small open truck. It was kind of like an old army jeep. The driver and an armed guard sat a couple of feet away, in front of him. They passed a bottle back and forth between them and were talking loudly. Neil closed his eyes when he saw the guard start to turn his head to look back and check on him.

His head throbbed and his body ached, and every bounce on the dirt road only added to his pains. But they were nothing compared to what he had already seen there. He felt charged with fear and impatience — his body was shrieking at him. He had to act fast and somehow get away.

The vehicle slowed and turned a corner. The buildings on either side were dark or dimly lit. They seemed to be in a part of the place where there were few people about at present. As the jeep gathered speed again, Neil pushed himself up with his feet and slipped over the side. He rolled on the ground, got some balance and rushed toward the shadows. A few seconds later he heard the squeal of brakes and a shout, just as he ducked around the corner. The unhappy sound of reverse gear.

Neil looked around. He was in another patch of open ground that was surrounded by ramshackle two-story wooden buildings. Spotlights swept the area methodically. He could see more guards stationed or walking patrol, no matter which direction he turned. There was nowhere to go, they would grab him in a minute if he tried to flee.

The building beside him was dark — and the door opened when Neil tried it. He slipped inside. There was no lock, but he was out of sight for the moment. He knew it was only a temporary refuge. Sooner or later he would be found if he stayed there. Then he heard a loud noise and felt the building shake briefly. The driver and guard were cursing unintelligibly, and then they began to laugh. In trying to take the corner they had backed into the building itself. From the window, he saw them glancing around. Then they drove off, apparently deciding that someone else would catch Neil.

He was safe, for now. He sank to the floor and sat in the darkness. It felt good to rest his back against the wall, to be alone. But his mind was still swarming with unbearable images and raging confusion.

And then he became aware of the mask again. It was still on his face. As soon as he thought about it, he could feel it seem to tighten, choking his pores as if it were trying to enter his body through his skin. Suppressing panic for a moment, Neil tried again to remove it. Be calm, he told himself, find an edge and work it back. But he got nowhere with it. He could feel his fingertips on it, he could even make a small portion of it move slightly — but then it always slipped away from his hand and back in place. It was impossibly filmy to his touch, but on his face it felt heavy and oppressive.

He finally gave up, sobbing once out loud and banging his head back against the wall in frustration.

Someone laughed.

Neil froze. The shocking human sound had come from only a few feet away. He could hardly think at all now, let alone know what to do. He heard the soft pat of childlike footsteps on the floor, followed by a very loud click, and then an overhead light went on. There were piles of clothes everywhere, the floor dotted with random heaps of them. Nothing but clothes. The woman grinning hideously at Neil was the same dwarf he had seen on the balustrade when he arrived at Marisa's house.

She was one of them, she would alert the guards —

The woman read his panic and immediately made calming gestures to stop him from doing anything foolish. Neil was thinking that he ought to kill her and turn the light off. Her voice sounded like that of a toy doll, but there was something soothing in her tone. She held her finger to her lips. Neil sat where he was. It occurred to him that he was dead anyway, so what was the point of resisting, much less killing someone else? He felt tired. All of the energy he had somehow summoned up in escaping from the guards and then hiding in this barnlike building was now gone. His head ached and the mask felt like a huge clamp on his face. Let it be. Roll into it.

Noise, the sound of activity outside. The woman went to the window to take a look, then quickly turned away. She gestured with her hand for Neil to follow her. They went up a large, open flight of stairs to the second floor, which was covered with more mounds of clothing. There was no sorting, no order, just random tilting piles of ordinary clothes, as if they had simply been thrown down where they were.

The woman kept gesturing and Neil followed her to the front side of the building. There were two windows overlooking the open ground outside. She went to one and pointed Neil to the other. He no longer thought of her as a threat to him, and yet he didn't feel that she was a friend or ally. This place was like a concentration camp, but without the Nazis. The dwarf woman was perhaps a prisoner, but one allowed to live because of the work she did with these clothes, or because someone liked her — some insane reason. He didn't know, he had no idea, just fleeting guesses.

Why was he there?

Dozens of guards had assembled in the yard outside. The spotlights were fixed, illuminating the whole area in a harsh light. Everyone seemed to be standing around expectantly. Neil could feel the sense of something about to happen, and yet it was such an utterly barren scene — his novelist's instinct found it completely unworthy. Of anything.

A moment later, three large trucks arrived, each one full of women. They ranged from teenagers to the elderly. The guards immediately swung into action, pulling or flinging the women off the trucks. The older women were dealt with summarily, either shot in the head, stabbed or clubbed to the ground. Within moments, there were bodies everywhere and the spurious air of order had given way to chaos and mayhem.

It was worse for middle-aged women. Guards hacked at their skulls with axes, chopping off clumps of hair and flesh. They were pulled out of their clothes, beaten, slashed and kicked. Long knives or wide swords were inserted into them, then twisted, and yanked. Pistols were roughly forced into their mouths, vaginas or anuses, and then fired. Ears and noses were slashed off before their deliverance.

Neil sagged against the window frame. He gazed at the guards who were doing all of this. They didn't look angry, so much as determined. Like homeowners who had a job to do, because they could not bear to live with a certain pest. Whether you sprayed them in groups or crushed them beneath your heel one at a time, they had to go.

Two guards held a woman face down on the ground. Another guard pulled her hair so that her head was raised up a few inches. A fourth guard came and stood over her. He had some tool in his hand. A saw. He began to saw the back of her neck, like a log. The woman's body quivered like wire strung too tight, electric, and then collapsed. The guard swung her loose head and rolled it away like a bowling ball.

The youngest fared worst of all, their breasts hacked off, knives thrust into them, their loins doused with gasoline and set afire. Or they were fucked first, repeatedly, until someone decided they were no longer worthy. He saw one girl held bent over at the waist and entered from behind. When the guard in her was about to climax, he waved his fingers excitedly in the air. Another guard stepped up, swung a hatchet and decapitated the girl. It wasn't clean, it took three blows, but that only seemed to enhance the pleasure of the one who was coming in her. Then the guard with the bloody hatchet held up the girl's head and pushed her lips back to expose her teeth — evoking loud cheers and laughter. She had long straight hair, parted in the middle. A style that would fit in easily in Rome, Paris, London, New York or San Francisco.

Neil turned to the dwarf woman perched on a pile of clothes at the other window. It was as if he wasn't there. Her expression was blank, but she was totally caught up in what she was seeing. She gazed outward, like someone watching the crucial scene in a gripping movie. Understandable, and yet — how could *anyone* watch *that?*

Neil had felt such fear, but now he saw fear as something shallow, a surface ripple. In his blood and in his bones, in his whole body, he felt his own death now, and he knew it didn't matter. Not even to him.

He looked outside once more. It was like a Bosch painting, except that Bosch lacked the imagination or nerve for this horror. In some forlorn part of his brain Neil heard Abba singing "Fernando" in a tinny voice. And there, almost directly below him — he saw Marisa. She was watching the

scene, close up. She was in a group of six or eight people, all
of whom wore civilian garb. She had on a long black dress
and leather coat. Her hair was done up in braids that were
coiled tightly to her head.

Marisa...

The dwarf woman gagged and giggled.

Marisa turned and rested her head on the shoulder of
the young man standing beside her. His arm went around
her, then rubbed her shoulders and back comfortingly. She
looked up and he kissed her. No doubt about it, Neil was
certain that it was the young man he had seen in the alcove,
the same one who had knocked him out with a blackjack.

A little implosion, that's all.

Opera.

Neil turned and ran.

⇒ 17 ⇐

Miserere

As if he should be surprised! Neil felt angry at himself. He had seen Father Anton at work. If her uncle, a priest, could be implicated in this, how could Marisa not be? Still, it was crushing to see her out there, calmly taking everything in. Kissing her lover. Was that Hugo?

The dwarf woman called out to him. Neil's foot snagged and he fell onto a large pile of clothing. He rolled over and came to rest, lying on his back. For a moment he thought he might never move again. He wanted only to remain there, burrowing in, hiding in the drifts of old clothes. He inhaled deeply. He could detect the whole range of human smells that lingered in the dresses, skirts and blouses, even terror and death.

He closed his eyes, allowing himself to imagine for just a second that when he opened them again he would be somewhere else. In the Italy that he knew. In his car, which worked. On a road, to somewhere.

But where was the house, where was his car?

What had happened to him?

He opened his eyes and saw the dwarf woman smiling down at him. But she wagged her finger and shook her head. Neil understood. She was right. If he just ran impulsively like that, he would inevitably give himself away and soon be captured. That wasn't the way to do it. Neil nodded in agreement and almost managed a faint smile.

She had seemed positively deranged the first time he had encountered her, but now he understood the mad, antic gleam in her eyes, the grinning and harsh laughter. He was where she lived.

The woman took his thumb in her pudgy little hand and tugged. Neil pushed himself to his feet. Outside, the screams and gunshots continued. He followed the woman through the mounds of clothing, toward the back of the upper room. It was much darker there, no windows, no electric light. They came to a door in the side wall. She opened it. Neil saw stairs disappearing down into complete darkness. No, he didn't like that.

The woman made a series of gestures, and Neil realized that she was trying to give him directions, to tell him which way to go. To escape? What else could it be? She would have called the guards and turned him in by now if that was her intention. She pointed to the front of the room and held her hand to her ear — Neil noticed that the sounds of the bloody rampage outside were slowly diminishing. The woman was telling him to hurry now, while so many of the guards were still preoccupied. This was his best opportunity. Okay, he understood. The directions were simple, which probably meant that his chances were almost nil. But he would try.

He stepped through the doorway and turned to nod appreciatively to the woman. Her head bobbed, she waved, urging him to go, and she closed the door. Neil put his hand on the wall and made his way slowly down the stairs in complete darkness. He had no trouble and he found the door at the bottom. He listened carefully for a few seconds, and heard nothing but the muffled sounds from outside.

The door opened directly into the adjacent building. The room was dark, but enough light penetrated from the front windows. Neil saw that this building was almost identical to the one he had just left. A large room and piles of clothing — though they were smaller and fewer in number. He moved quickly to the far side of the room, at the back. He found the next door that he was looking for, but it wasn't where it was supposed to be. He expected to find a door that would let him out at the rear of the building, but this door was in the side wall again and it clearly led into the next building. Neil wondered if he had misunderstood the woman. He must have. Well, he had no choice but to go on.

The ground floor room in the next building contained dozens of bunks, cots and bed mats on the floor. They looked too mean and wretched to be for the guards. But there were no inmates, the beds were all empty. The room was bathed in the same eerie grey-white light from outside. Neil hurried to the other rear corner. He groaned aloud when he discovered that once again the door was in the side wall. Then he noticed the quiet — there was no more gunfire. He had to keep going, and hurry.

He opened the door a crack and saw that there were lights on in the next room. His view was blocked by a wood partition. He opened the door a little more and eased himself quietly inside. There was a strong smell of alcohol in the air. Then he heard the sound of someone moving about. Neil had never fought with anybody in his life, not even in grammar school in Southie — a remarkable but, he sometimes felt, dubious achievement. One person he could deal with — *maybe*. Two or more? Ha ha.

Then he saw it, on the other side of the room — the door in the back wall, the door he needed, to get outside. It was about thirty feet away. Neil stared at it. The floor was bare, aside from a few small wood crates and boxes lying about. There was nothing at all between him and the door that he could crawl behind or use to hide himself if he had to.

Neil moved carefully and slowly, testing each step, edging along the partition. The sounds he heard were slight, impossible to figure. He inched his face along the wood. Then a sigh, and a woman's voice, just a few words that were answered briefly by another woman. Neil was puzzled by this, but also vaguely encouraged. If these women were prisoners too, like the dwarf, they might be willing to help him.

Neil crouched and slowly expanded his angle of vision into the room. He saw some worktables that were cluttered with jars, boxes, hand tools and clumps of packing straw. Then the back of a woman's head came into view, grey hair tied up in a bun. She was seated on the other side of the tables, her back to Neil.

He leaned a little farther beyond the partition and saw the other woman, also grey-haired. She was bent over, apparently engaged in some chore. She was about ten feet away from the woman seated by the tables. Two older women. It occurred to Neil that they could be sorting out and packing up any valuables taken from the victims, like coins and rings. If that was the case, there might well be a guard in the room, watching them, still out of Neil's sight.

But then the woman straightened up and he recognized her as one of Marisa's relatives, her mother or one of her grandmothers. So the other one, with her back to Neil, was probably also a relative. Of course, they were all in on this madness. That seemed to make it a little less likely that there was a guard with them.

Neil took a deep breath and stepped around the partition — it was the back wall of some wooden shelves. He scanned the room quickly, saw that there was no guard, just the two women. He moved around the worktables. There were no front windows — an unexpected help. The women looked at him, then at each other, and they began to laugh. Neil stopped as if he had run into a brick wall. The open floor of the large room was strewn with the dead bodies of small children. There were dozens of them, boys and girls, infants and toddlers, some dressed, some naked, their skin color ranging from bone white to a pale grey-blue.

The old woman who was seated on a long bench was the grandmother who had been sharpening fruit spoons. In fact, she had one of those spoons in her hand now. On the bench beside her was the body of a small girl, her head resting on the woman's lap. They were laughing louder now. The woman pushed the girl's eyelid back and deftly used the spoon to scoop out the eye, which she then held out for Neil to see. He couldn't move. Then she reached toward the table, turned the spoon and dropped the eye into a large glass jar of clear liquid — the alcohol. There were already dozens of eyes in the jar, like shiny blue and brown pearls. Neil saw two other jars on the table, full and capped. He looked at the bodies on the floor and saw those that had been done — their empty eye sockets dark, thin strands of fleshy membrane trailing across their faces. And the rest, all around him, waiting.

He felt like a piece of ice, or stone, but he walked carefully toward the woman on the bench. She was still laughing, but her eyes were watchful. As he drew closer, she stood up and quickly scooted a few yards away. The child's head thumped on the bench, and then the body slid off. Neil went to the worktable. And there was grandma's favorite set of spoons, a dozen or fifteen of them, in different sizes. He took one in his hand and ran his finger along the edge. Sharp enough for the grisly work at hand, but was it sharp enough for him?

Neil put the spoon in his pocket and, without even glancing at the two women, went quickly to the back of the room. He opened the door, slipped outside and looked around. Arcs of light, moving zones of exposed ground. But there were also wide, shifting pockets of darkness, and Neil ran into the darkness. He expected to feel a bullet in his back at any moment. He kept running, veering off, swerving back, always hugging the darkness.

No alarms went off, no shots were fired, but Neil had a sense that he wasn't going to make it. His breath was ragged now, his chest and legs were tightening in pain, and a cramp was stitching through his abdomen. He kept on, gasping loudly but driving himself forward. Don't stop.

Then he hit the fence. Barbed wire raked across his scalp and dug into his throat, belly and thighs. He bounced back, hit the ground, and now he couldn't move. He couldn't even breathe. Flat on his back — there was the moon again. It wasn't his asthma, he realized. He'd had the wind knocked out of him, but that was all. Slowly his chest began to move again — oh, the sweet, sweet taste of air.

But he knew that the light would find him soon, he had to move. Neil dragged himself under the fence. Another twenty tortuous yards of dangerous open ground, and then he was in the woods, safe for the moment. He tried to follow the general direction the dwarf woman had indicated. Before long, however, he could sense the river nearby, and that was all he needed. For a few minutes he stumbled around, struggling in the darkness with thick brush, saplings and swampy ground underfoot. Finally, Neil found a clear patch of solid land at the water's edge. He sat down to let his body rest.

The idea was to swim to the other side and thereby escape. But what was on the other side? *Where* was the other side? The river looked so wide that he doubted he could make it across. What if he gave up and surrendered? If he begged to see Marisa, would she come? Would she recognize him, and save his life? But Neil immediately felt a sense of shame and anger. How could he even even consider that possibility? He had seen her world, and the only alternatives were to flee or to die.

He took the spoon out of his pocket and began to scrape his face with the edge of it. He dug in hard, not caring when he felt pain and his own fresh blood. Then the pain blossomed across his face and into his head, and he had a sense that he was breaking the mask in places. Hope electrified him and he gouged at his cheeks and chin and forehead even more energetically. It was like fire breaking out in his skin and then penetrating his brain. He bent over in agony. The spoon fell from his hand.

He saw the water in front of him and it looked so sweet and soothing. That was where he was supposed to go. The other side. He waded in and began to swim. Cold, too cold. But he didn't care. Neil swept his arms and kicked feebly. Then the body of a dead man bumped into him. He pushed it away, but another one bobbed against him, and another, and suddenly he saw that he was surrounded by countless bodies floating in the river. They moved slowly, drifting along at the edge of the current.

Go with them.

No...

You're one of them.

No...

You are. This is where pain ends.

No. Let someone else kill me. I want to see it happen. Neil turned and splashed his way back to land. He dragged himself under a clump of thick bushes and nestled close to the ground, curled up protectively. His face felt as if it had long jagged strips of raw exposed flesh. Had Neil broken the mask, ripped parts of it away? He couldn't tell. His brain wouldn't focus on anything, and that didn't even bother him. He didn't care anymore. He was so cold and wet, and he had nothing left.

⇒ 18 ⇐

Revival

Neil shivered so violently it seemed as if his whole body was trying to shake itself to pieces. His clothes were wet, clinging to him. He felt the dank cold deep in his bones. His limbs were stiff and had no strength. He was on the ground, lying in tall grass.

Daylight. So much easier for someone to see him. At first he thought it was morning, but when he cautiously raised his head and looked around, Neil saw the big house — Marisa's house — shimmering with golden light. It must be late afternoon. He felt a tremendous sense of relief, but it was soon followed by a wave of confusion. How had he come to be there, outside the front of the house, and at this hour of the day? What had happened to him last night? Why had Marisa left him? Where was she?

The mask — fear and panic boiled up in Neil again as he realized that the mask was still on his face. For a brief moment, he had begun to consider the possibility that everything he'd experienced there had been nothing more than a long bizarre hallucination, or dream. That he had arrived there, fallen into a mysterious trance or had a brain seizure that somehow unleashed him on a journey into deep corners of his own subconscious mind. That seemed unlikely, and the presence of the mask disproved it.

Unless the mask was merely another imaginary sign of his continuing mental breakdown. Is this dementia?

Neil stood up and looked back, away from the house. He saw his car, still where he had left it. The hood was raised and the front end was partly dismantled. He moved a few steps to get a better angle and then he could see the radiator lying on the ground. That appeared to clinch it. There was no way Neil would have tried to take the radiator out by himself. He wasn't mechanically adept, he had no tools with him, and there was no point to it, especially in this remote spot. Someone else had done it, Marisa's workman, just as Neil remembered.

But he also noticed that the cluster of shacks and huts visible on the nearest ridge were half-collapsed, with doors gone or hanging loose, roofs caved in, all of them utterly dilapidated. No one lived or worked in them. And the grounds immediately around the house looked even more overgrown with weeds and brush than he seemed to remember — thick coils of brambles and briars sprawled about, slowly spreading, creating impenetrable thickets around the building.

The windows were gone — another small shock. The sun still caught the tiles and lit them brilliantly, but all of the windows were vacant, dark and empty rectangles in the face of the house. In some of the frames he could see jagged shards of glass that hadn't yet fallen away, but most of the glass was gone. So was the front door — not just open, but gone. The house stood open to the elements, and to anyone who happened to come there.

Like him. Neil walked along the crumbling balustrade, gazing at the old house and its surroundings. There was no sign of human life anywhere, nor any indication that there had been for many years. Again he wondered if he had somehow imagined everything — Marisa, her family, the workmen, the passion and fantastic sex, the billiards room, the cellar, the wagon, the horror and savagery he had seen. If only he had imagined all that. It was just a big crazy dream. Ha ha.

But how could he have conjured up all those peculiar details, like the bird skulls in the stew? And the sensory memories that were still so vivid to him — how it felt to be inside Marisa, the touch of her wet mouth on his skin? No, it wasn't possible. Besides, his car and the awful weight on his face told him it was something else, something unfinished.

Neil hesitated. He glanced back toward his car again. He could just walk away. Follow the gravel road until it brought him to another road, take that one and keep going until he either flagged down a passing car or reached the next town.

Then find a doctor — please take this thing off my face.

No. Not yet. He walked into the house. It was gloomy, but enough sunlight reached the interior for Neil to find his way around. Instead of going upstairs and trying to get to the bedroom where his things were, he began to check the ground floor rooms. The house was silent, except for the rush and swirl of the mountain wind as it blew through the corridors and passageways, which only added to the feeling of emptiness.

He went through several rooms that were almost bare, containing a few pieces of rotting furniture. The floors were littered with broken glass, grey grit, and mats of damp dust. Paper wasp nests clung to the upper walls, the empty ceiling fixtures and dangling sconces. Wide bands of wallpaper had peeled off and crumpled to the floors.

So far, everything he saw argued that the house had been abandoned years before. But he couldn't be sure yet. These might be some of the rooms that had been left unused by the family, as Marisa had explained to Neil. He was beginning to think that he would find nobody, but he also believed that he would find *something* — something that made sense of all this to him.

Then Neil opened a door and recognized the dining room. The long table and the sideboards were gone, but some of the chairs remained, dusty and scattered, lying on their sides. The wall tapestries were shredded and black with mildew. It was impossible to imagine that anyone had eaten there in years.

Neil walked quickly to the far end of the room, opened the door and made his way along the short, unlit passage. The windows in the billiards room were shuttered on the inside, but thin lines of fading daylight allowed him to make out various objects in the prevailing gloom. The billiards table was still there, and apparently in good condition. It startled Neil to see the sofa where he and Marisa had spent time. And the little television, the radio. Even their wine glasses — he stood frozen, staring at them. Finally, he went closer and lifted one. A small pool of red wine swirled at the bottom. Neil immediately recognized the strong tannic bouquet.

It was no dream or hallucination — none of what he had seen — unless he was experiencing it all again. Or it had never ended. The mask was still on his face, after all. But the mask didn't explain anything. He'd encountered the dwarf woman, Marisa, the workers and servants, Marisa's family — all of that — well before they got to the masks. Neil felt like a dog chasing his own tail. It was a waste of time. It wasn't possible to make sense of experiences that seemed to arise from some lost pocket of reality, a place that had its own logic and reason — all of which escaped him. He had the irrational feeling of being caught in someone else's dream world. But that would mean he had no chance of escape, which he knew was absurd.

He turned the television on, but the screen stayed dark and there was no sound. The generator was off. He tried the radio, and the sexy, breathless voice of a woman singing in French squiggled out of nowhere. Neil laughed. There were batteries in the radio, and they still worked. He almost switched it off, but didn't. The radio station and the song reminded him that there was still an outside world. *His* world. He increased the volume, and it sounded good, it was like bright light and fresh air.

Neil picked up the box of matches Marisa had used and lit a candle. He carried it with him as he crossed the room and ascended the circular iron staircase to the second floor. In the corridor, he turned and made his way to the bedroom he had used. The door was closed. Before he tried to open it, he went into the bathroom. His toiletries were missing.

Neil looked in the mirror and saw himself — bruises and lumps on the side of the head, scratches, crusted spots of blood, all the signs and marks of what he had experienced. And his features were subtly different, younger and smoother, but also more drawn, tightened, as if with pain and deep inner hurt. He scared himself. The mask. He turned quickly away.

The bedroom was different. The furniture was still there, each item exactly where he remembered it. But there were no sheets on the bed and no blanket. Neil's things were gone — his overnight bag, the shirt and jeans he'd left out, the Rose Tremain novel he was reading — all gone.

Movement — he heard a sound outside. More than one — there were sounds in the house, both above and below him. Neil cupped his hand around the candle and walked quickly back into the main corridor. He saw the faint blue glow down the corridor at once.

As he approached the alcove, one of the servant women came down the steps into the corridor and walked right past him without a glance, as if he didn't exist. Now he even heard the sound of people outside, carried through the open window at the end of the corridor. Nothing unusual, just the distant, ordinary sounds of people at work, talking among themselves.

The young man was in the bunk. The same young man he had seen the first time there, and who had struck him with a blackjack, and who had kissed Marisa at the scene of that unspeakable atrocity. But now he wore the black uniform Neil recognized. It was not the uniform of any police force or army, at least none that he could recognize, but it only seemed the more frightening for its lack of definition.

The young man's skin was bone white, puckering at the corners of his mouth and eyes. His body didn't move at all, there was no sign of breathing. Neil grasped one hand and felt for a pulse. Nothing. He let it drop back onto the black-clad shirt. The blue votive candle flames danced in a brief flick of the wind.

Neil was about to turn away, but he saw the young man's face seem to turn ruddier, flushed with sudden color. The slack skin on the face tightened, the chest rose slightly, and a soft sigh of breath broke the silence. Neil could not move. The eyes opened, and turned.

The handsome young man smiled as he reached for Neil.

⇒ 19 ⇐

Zuzu

Neil backed away instinctively, but then he noticed the expression on the face of Marisa's lover: his smile was warm and loving, his eyes were filled with — gratitude? His hands grasped feebly at Neil's arm and then his cold fingers brushed Neil's skin and rubbed his palm tenderly.

Neil yanked his hand away. The candle slipped out of his grip and was extinguished when it hit the floor. Now the tiny space was lit only by the votive candles, the air suddenly colored a chilly blue. He was fascinated and horrifed by the look of pain and sorrow on the young man's face. It was as if he could not bear to be parted from Neil's touch.

Fear and hatred welled up within him. Neil lunged forward, grabbed the young man's throat and began to squeeze as hard as he could. But now Marisa's lover smiled gratefully up at him again. His eyes blazed with light, his smooth cheeks glowed with a rush of life and color. Neil felt a terrifying sensation, as if his own strength and energy were flowing through his hands, into the body of Marisa's lover, who was gaining vitality and starting to push himself up from the bunk.

Neil forced him back down, and moved away. A hand gripped his shoulder. He shook it off and spun around. Father Panic. The old priest grinned at him. Then he spread his arms wide and stepped closer, as if to take Neil in a comforting paternal embrace. The alcove seemed impossibly small, a death-box in which he was trapped. He could feel Marisa's lover behind him, clutching and tugging at his shirt.

He shoved the priest back against the wall in the landing and rushed past him, down the short flight of stairs, into the dark corridor. Neil's brain teemed with confused thoughts. It seemed as if his presence alone brought these people back. Were they real in themselves or was his deranged mind creating them before his very eyes? He had to get out of the house as fast as possible, and then far away from there.

"Ustashas!" Somewhere outside but close by, men shouted gleefully and triumphantly. "Ustashas! Ustashas!" Then he heard gunfire. Had war somehow broken out in Italy and fighting engulfed even this unlikely corner of the Marches? But that was an absurd idea. The madness was *here,* either a part of this house or a part of himself.

Neil felt trapped on the second floor. He heard the sounds of Father Panic and Marisa's lover in the alcove. The only sure quick way he knew to get out was back down the circular staircase into the billiards room. He shut the door tight and then descended the stairs as fast as he could. It wasn't until he reached the bottom step that he noticed that the lamps were all on and dozens of candles were lit, filling the room with a warm soft glow. As Neil walked slowly toward the bar he realized that all the shouts and sounds of movement about the house had vanished. The only thing he heard now was music, a dreamy mindless techno burble from the radio.

The television was on, but silent. A handsome young man wearing only pajama bottoms and a sexy young woman in a revealing nightie were talking, their faces and gestures overly expressive. The stage set was meant to suggest an expensively decorated ultra-modern bedroom, but every-thing was so polished and tidy that it resembled a display in a furniture store. An episode from an Italian soap opera, Neil thought absently. Then the pretty couple on the screen hurled themselves into each other's arms, pressed their bod-ies tightly in a feverish embrace, mashed their open mouths together and tumbled backward onto a huge bed.

Marisa was stretched out on the sofa. She was wearing only a black bra and a half-slip, and the large blue opal that hung from a ribbon at the base of her throat. Her hair was wild, her eyes shiny, her mouth wet. She raised one leg, bent at the knee, and held her hand out to him. Turn around now and leave, or stay forever. Neil sat down beside her.

"My lover..."

"Take it off me."

"What?"

"The mask. Take it off my face."

"What mask? There is no mask."

"Please."

"Silly."

"Marisa, *please*."

"Zuzu."

"Zuzu..."

She smiled, caressing his cheek. "Kiss me."

"Let me go."

"No one is keeping you." She looked hurt, pouting, and she turned her face slightly to the side. "Go, if you want."

The sense of urgency and fear within him disappeared. He couldn't leave. She understood things he didn't, things he had to know. She was the only one who could show him the way — to anywhere, or nowhere. He felt as if he knew nothing, and she knew everything.

But even more than that, he wanted her again, he wanted to kiss her and touch her and enter her, be one with her. The room was golden, the air was sweet with her fragrance. He wanted to taste her again. He felt the heat from her body, like a deeply soothing radiance that reached into him, giving him comfort and peace. He put his hand on her thigh, his fingertips moving lightly over her beautiful skin.

She turned her head and smiled at him again. Neil kissed her and he felt her arms come around his shoulders. Their eyes closed as their tongues touched, their faces pressing together, skin to skin — mask to mask — and he felt once again as if they were a part of each other, sensation fusing them in a fire of infinite wholeness and pleasure.

He saw a child, a boy about seven or eight years old, dressed in rags, looking thin and frightened. Then a hand grabbed the boy's hair and jerked his head to one side.

Neil tried to open his eyes, but couldn't.

Marisa was dressed in black. She was the person holding the boy by the hair. Her face alive, wild. She swung a ball peen hammer into the back of the boy's skull, the crack of bone creating a million screaming fractures in Neil's nerves and brain.

Zuzu's mouth sucked at his — and he had the distant, almost abstract sensation of flying slowly into her.

The boy's blinking and vacant eyes were replaced by those of a girl about the same age. Her round face was gaunt and hollow. Her eyes closed and she turned her face away slightly, and then Marisa drove the axe blade into the back of the girl's neck, at the top of the spine.

He still couldn't open his eyes, nor could he pull his face away from hers. His body churned and he kicked violently. He pushed against her and rolled away, peeling her arms off him. His face felt as if it were being eaten and burned with acid as he broke away from her and fell off the sofa. Neil quickly got to his feet. She looked like a big cat, holding herself up half off the sofa, her arms straight, her hands flat on the floor. Zuzu grinned at him through the long black hair that hung across her face.

"My lover", she said. "Without me, you're lost."

Neil turned and ran, bouncing off the walls of the dark passage into the dining room, and then into the next room.

Broken glass cracked beneath his shoes. Open windows. Neil grabbed a sill, swung his body out and then let himself drop to the ground.

He didn't know which side of the house he was on. The air was grey and full of moisture. He was in a thick wet fog — *il morbo*. He could barely see five feet in front of him. Still he ran — staggered — as fast as he could in the circumstances, his eyes fixed on the ground just ahead. He hit saplings and tripped on rocks, pushed through thickets and crawled over rocky ridges that suddenly loomed before him, blocking his flight.

Finally he had to stop. He bent over, gasping for breath.

When he looked up, two men wearing black uniforms stood in front of him. They laughed as they took him in hand, and they didn't even bother to draw their pistols.

⇒20⇐
Grotta Rossa

They walked for some distance. Neil couldn't make out anything in the fog that swirled and blew around them, but the two guards knew where they were going. He tried to speak to them, a few words in Italian, and then German, but they merely laughed at him. Their hands were like iron clamps on his arms.

Neil's face was raw and the cold air grated painfully across his skin. He couldn't tell whether the mask still clung to him or not. In certain places it seemed to be gone, but he felt a lingering tightness and weight around the eyes and mouth. Nonetheless, it hardly seemed to matter anymore.

Real or not, there or gone, the mask was almost irrelevant to his situation now. The guards had him and could do whatever they wanted with him. He thought about resisting, struggling, perhaps breaking free and fleeing, but he sensed that it was useless to try. He would simply wander around in *il morbo* until he fell off a cliff or they caught him again.

Then they were on a smooth wide path, and a high stone outcropping in the side of a hill appeared before them. The guards force-walked Neil to a cleft in the rock, and then inside. Within a few yards the path turned, and they emerged in a large, roughly circular open area. A limestone massif ran through the Marches, Neil knew, and limestone lent itself particularly well to the formation of caverns.

They were in the grotto Marisa had mentioned to him. It was lit by mounted torches and banks of candles. There was a simple wooden altar on raised ground. Behind it stood a rusty iron cross that was taller than a man. A few plain benches served as pews. A narrow stream of water bubbled out of the rock and flowed in a cut channel through the makeshift chapel. There were several plaster statues of the Virgin Mary around the place, the largest of which stood beside the source of the stream. Mary's robes were blue and white, and her face was painted with unnaturally bright enamel colors — red lips, blue eyes, shiny white skin.

Several people sat on the benches and another group stood in a tight huddle behind the altar. Neil recognized Father Panic and other members of Marisa's family. Then he noticed a third group of people, in a side area that was not as well lit. They were the workers and farmhands, dressed in rough clothes or rags, kneeling submissively on the damp bare rock. There were a couple of dozen of them. Their heads were bowed, their hands clasped as if in prayer. He saw the dwarf woman. She was the only person in that group who knelt with her head up, looking around calmly. When she saw Neil she grinned maniacally at him, and then shook her head.

Guards were posted all around, but they looked relaxed and they had their pistols holstered. They stood, watching, waiting.

Neil was brought to the area between the benches and the altar, and forced to kneel beside the fast-moving stream of water. His hands were tied behind his back, and then his ankles as well.

The same lunacy again, Neil thought. A conversion and baptism, but then what? His only fear was that they might cut his tongue out, as he'd seen them do with others. Could he pre-empt it — if he recited the Apostles' Creed, for instance, demonstrating that he was already a Catholic? Neil was not even sure that he remembered all of the Apostles' Creed anymore, and he knew it only in English. But if they would listen to him again, if he had a few seconds to explain, appeal...

The circle of people behind the altar fanned out a little and gazed at him. Father Panic in his vestments, Marisa in a black blouse and black skirt that reached just below her knees. Her lover, also in uniform. A few guards and older people stood with them. She looked so young and beautiful — but the sinister black uniform made her look like a girl scout from hell.

Neil watched her hopefully. When Marisa finally looked directly at him, her expression showed no flicker of recognition, or even of interest in who he was or what was happening. She turned her head and spoke quietly with the young man, who smiled, nodded and replied to her. Neil opened his mouth to address her by name, but a guard immediately shoved a thick rag between his teeth, rammed it halfway down his throat. A bitter alkaline taste filled Neil's nostrils and lungs — it was the same hideous fungus that he had experienced in the box room. He began to gag, trying desperately to spit, push and force the cloth out of his mouth. His body jumped wildly but the guards held him in place.

The handsome young man turned slightly and reached down to pick up something from the floor behind him. It was a wooden box with leather straps and metal bolts. He came forward and shoved the strange device over Neil's head. The straps were cinched tight under his throat. The bolts were turned — and Neil felt flat metals plates tighten against the sides and back of his skull. He could hardly breathe, his lungs were in extreme distress. His brain reeled. Then men were grunting close around him as they turned the bolts forcefully, relentlessly.

The last thing Neil heard — before he felt the bones in his head begin to crunch and splinter — was the sound of men and women laughing.

Notes

1. In an apparent attempt to ape the Germans, the [Croatian] Ustashas set up a number of concentration camps. Being far less organized than their mentors, or lacking the technology, they often resorted in these camps to knives with which to murder Serbs, Jews, Gypsies and undesirable Croats. The most infamous camp was at Jasenovac on the Sava river, on the border of Bosnia. Tim Judah, *The Serbs: History, Myth & the Destruction of Yugoslavia* (Yale University Press, 1997).

2. Seven hundred thousand men, women and children were killed there alone in ways that made even the hair of the Reich's experts stand on end, as some of them are said to have admitted when they were amongst themselves. The preferred instruments of execution were saws and sabres, axes and hammers, and leather cuff-bands with fixed blades that were fastened on the lower arm and made especially in Solingen for the purpose of cutting throats, as well as a kind of rudimentary crossbar gallows on which the Serbs, Jews and Bosnians, once rounded up, were hanged in rows like crows or magpies. Not far from Jasenovac, in a radius of no more than ten miles, there were also the camps of Prijedor, Stara Gradiska and Banja Luka, where the Croatian militia, its hand strengthened by the Wehrmacht and its spirit by the Catholic church, performed one day's work after another in similar manner. The history of this massacre, which went on for years, is recorded in fifty thousand documents abandoned by the Germans and Croats in 1945... W.G. Sebald, *The Rings of Saturn,* translated by Michael Hulse (New Directions, 1998).

3. In *Kaputt,* his memoir of World War II, the Italian journalist Curzio Malaparte recounts the following incident, when he and Raffaele Casertano, then the Italian minister in Zagreb, met Ante Pavelic, the Poglavnik (*fuhrer,* or leader) of the Croatian forces:
   "While he spoke, I gazed at a wicker basket on the Poglavnik's desk. The lid was raised and the basket seemed to be filled with

mussels, or shelled oysters — as they are occasionally displayed in the windows of Fortnum and Mason in Piccadilly in London. Casertano looked at me and winked.

"'Would you like a nice oyster stew?'

"'Are they Dalmatian oysters?' I asked the Poglavnik.

"Ante Pavelic removed the lid from the basket and revealed the mussels, that slimy and jelly-like mass, and he said, smiling, with that tired good-natured smile of his, 'It is a present from my loyal *ustashis*. Forty pounds of human eyes.'" Curzio Malaparte, *Kaputt*, translated by Cesare Foligno (E. P. Dutton, 1946).